SMII

This book is a work of fiction. Names, characters, organisations, places, events and incidents are either products of the author's imagination or are used fictitiously.

John Gammon Series four Book One

Another case for Detective Inspector John Gammon.
A thriller based in the Peak District of Derbyshire. John has an unfinished serial killer case to solve and with the Peak District media challenging Bixton Police's abilities DI Gammon was under pressure.

A big thank you to the team behind getting my books to the publishing stage.
Martyn Wright possibly one of the best book cover designers available today who also markets the books through social media and local magazines and newspapers.

SMILE

Also a big thank you to the new recruit to the team Amanda Kiernan who stepped in to take over from the previous proof reader at short notice on the book "Let's Dance in The Kitchen" and now settled into doing the work with this next book " Smile" Thanks Amanda. Both of you are really very much appreciated.

John Gammon Series four Book One

Book sixteen in the John Gammon Peak District Detective books. This book follows on from "THE MEANING STONES"
In this latest book we find John Gammon in spiralling depression with murders unsolved and his sister also missing. John will need to conjure up all his abilities as a detective as well as a human being to get through this.
Colin J Galtrey books are sold throughout the world from the UK to France, Germany, Italy, Australia, North America etc
Take the opportunity to visit his Website www.colingaltrey.co.uk
Not your standard author with not only the John Gammon books but a series of other genres such as the books involving

SMILE

Gilbraith Drake and his friend Harriet
Weet these books are thrillers with help
from the after- life. Do you believe? If not
you may well do after reading "I AM
FAWN JONES" and "CALMING FARM"
Colin also wrote about two Irish lads and
the day they got the wrong side of the IRA
leaving one of them to make a choice that
will change their lives forever in "Scarab
Falls"
Enjoy the Trilogy "LOOKING FOR
SHONA" "THE HURT OF YOCHANA"
and "GROVE". A whirlwind set of books
set in Ireland, Scotland France and many
more places while the truth for the Egan
family is searched and finally revealed.
Read about a girl on the run from the
Mafia in "Got to Keep Running" She is in

fear for her life so she hides away in Cornwall and Derbyshire will she survive? The very latest book "Let's Dance in the Kitchen" Set during World War one and World War two. A love story involving two best friends and one woman and all the consequences this tragedy brings.

SMILE

Chapter 1

John had called Bixton police and PC
Magic, who had also volunteered to work
Christmas for Di Trimble, told John that
not ten minutes before, a man had called
the station to say that DI Gammon would
be calling and to let you know hole
thirteen is unlucky for some at Applegate
Golf Course in Derby.

"Magic, phone Derby police and tell them
to send forensics to the golf course, tell
them what you have told me and that I am
on my way". "Will do Sir. "I'm sorry for
ruining you and your family's day Sheba"
she hugged him and told him to go and do
what he had to. The poor girl didn't know
the full story behind the eye present John
had opened or John's concern that
somebody other than Sheba's family had

planted it under the tree. By default, that meant somebody had been in Sheba's house.

John headed for the golf course in total fear at what he might find. Derby police and forensics were there when John arrived; he flashed his warrant card at the PC on the entrance to the golf club. The course was deserted when he arrived at hole number thirteen. The white incident tent was up and Gammon spoke with DI Brown who he knew slightly from police functions over the years.

"What we got DI Brown?"

"Gruesome, worst thing I have seen in nearly thirty years on the force, this poor girl must have suffered in an unbelievable manner"

SMILE

"Why?" "Well, it appears she has no tongue".

John felt physically sick.

"Her eyes have been removed then it appears she was beaten then wrapped in cling film so she eventually suffocated to death. What sort of world are we living in John?"

Gammon couldn't speak, he felt anger and grief at the same time.

"We will have a full report for you by 9.00 am in the morning or do you want to hang on until after Boxing Day"?

"No, send it through I will be in work".

"Ok John, well there is little you can do here, go and enjoy your Christmas Day John".

DI Brown wasn't aware that the victim was John's sister Fleur. As he drove back he had tears rolling down his cheeks, the anger he felt toward the Lund family had reared again and in his mind, he owed his sister, this wasn't the policeman thinking this was the man who had lost the final strand of his family.

John's heart was heavy with grief, after thinking he had no family Fleur came into his life only to now leave it in such an awful way. He sat looking over his back garden, it was not a great Christmas he thought.

Fleur had confided in John that Sheridan was a very close associate of the gang Brian Lund had left behind, revenge was going to be theirs and by taking Fleur, which he believed they had, they had succeeded yet again at devastating John's life.

SMILE

Unknown to John, Fleur had a necklace with a pendant and inside were his contact details. It was DI Smarty with DCI Burns that knocked on John's door that Sunday morning, a knock John had done many times during his career knowing what he was about to say would change their life forever.

For some reason the loss of Fleur seemed so hard to take. He hadn't got to know her like he wanted because of both their commitments but she had always been there for him, now he was on his own again, life just seemed so cruel. He sat thinking and remembered something his genetic father had told him about life, he said "Life is like a jigsaw puzzle, what do you do if you have nearly finished it and the dog knocks it on the floor? Now you have a choice get up and walk away or pick up the pieces and start again" John mumbled to himself "Gammon start again"

He showered, dressed and headed into work.

Sorry to hear about your sister John one or two said as he walked in. It was good that people cared but he also wanted some private time. Fleur's body had been found at a golf course near Derby, she had been tortured then her body was shrink wrapped which obviously suffocated her. Wally said it must have been a horrendous death.

"Good Morning John although I doubt there is any good in your heart at the moment"

"No there isn't Heather, MI5 and MI6 let me down and Fleur"

SMILE

"Come into my office John".

Heather got John his usual strong black coffee.

"I have been notified by the Home Secretary that MI5 and MI6 will be putting the death of Fleur Dubois on the back burner whilst they try and conclude their case against Chico Lund and his associates. We can't expect any further help from them and I have been told that under no circumstances must my officers be allowed to jeopardise their case".

Heather, she was one of them, one of their own and they put her aside like a piece of road kill.

"This is unbelievable it really is".

"Look if you need some time off John that's fine by me"

"No, I have the dice case to crack and besides, what would I do all day"?

They all left to enjoy their Christmas break but John stayed at work. He stood with his coffee looking towards Losehill then realised he hadn't spoken to Saron to tell her about Fleur, he rang and the pub sounded busy.

"Hi John, thought you might have called Christmas night"

"Sorry Saron but we found Fleur brutally murdered in Derby" John didn't want to go over the grisly details over the phone so he said he would call around 4.00pm.

He stood thinking who would have known he was going to Sheba's for Christmas dinner so he rang Sheba and told her what had happened to Fleur. She was horrified.

SMILE

"Sheba who knew I was coming for lunch?"

"Well me of course, my Mum and Dad and my sister but I didn't tell her until five minutes before you arrived, why John?"

"Somebody had to know I was coming to yours to break in and plant that eye Sheba".

"Pretty sure Mum and Dad wouldn't have said anything, they hardly go out"

"Ok, just a thought".

"Pop over if you are feeling a bit down".

"I'm ok, I'm going to throw myself into the case, I owe Fleur that much Sheba".

"Well you know where I am when you need me" and she hung up.

Next John called DI Finney, he had been on watch with DI Stampfer on Christmas Day and with everything that happened the last person on his mind was Harry Salt the surveillance suspect.

Finney confirmed that Salt never left the house on Christmas Day on his shift and Tom Stampfer had said the same. John was feeling consumed with hatred for Chico Lund and his gang but he had to prove involvement.

Driving up to see Saron he felt low, maybe she could pick him up. Saron was sat at the bar waiting dressed in skin tight light blue jeans a pair of brown ankle boots and a dark blue blouse complemented with a Blue John necklace. She got off the stool and put her arm's round John.

"I'm so sorry for your loss John" He had all on not getting emotional, he cleared his throat and thanked her.

SMILE

"Get John a pint please Kathy", "coming up".

"New bar staff"?

"She has been working for us for about three weeks now, she was originally from Manchester, her name is Kathy Vickers, she moved down here with her job, she works at Rolls Royce in Derby, I think she is a metallurgist. Nice girl and very efficient behind the bar, plus it drags a few of the young lads in when she is on, you have to have a few tactics in this game John".

"Anyway, going back to Christmas Day, before then did you mention to anyone that I was having Christmas dinner at Sheba Filey's"?

"Only to Donna in passing, she was cooking to give me a break and she asked if you were coming"

"Were you in the bar when she asked"?

"Yes, I think so". "Can you remember if anybody else was sat at the bar or within ear shot"? Saron paused of a minute.

"John, there was a guy, he has been in a lot lately, now what did he say his name was? I know he gives me the creeps, he is about fifty I'm guessing with a Southern accent". "Think Saron"." Doug, oh hell my memory, Falham, Doug Falham".

Suddenly a light went on in John's head.

"Bloody hell Saron, Mickey Falham was a guy who lost a shed load of money on a betting scam, his wife took her own life and because the scam was run by some unsavoury people we were told to back off

SMILE

with any convictions because Special Ops were working on the bigger picture, I had the job of telling Falham that there would be no conviction at that time. Well he went mental, he said he lost his business his house, his wife committed suicide and I heard he had his son taken off him and put into care. About four years later he also took his own life. Could this Douglas Falham be his son? What nights does this guy come in"? "Probably be in about 9.00pm tonight John".

"Right, I'm going back to work to see what I can dig up on this guy, call me if he comes in please". "Of course John".

"Thanks" and John left Saron hoping he could be on to something.

John rushed back to Bixton, DI Lee called to say there was nothing on Harry Salt, he said he went a walk but that he followed him and he was soon back home and DS Yap was now on watch and they would report tomorrow as Gammon said he would do the next two days and DI Milton the nights.

Gammon sat at his desk looking through old cases and found that Mickey Falham had actually left a note condemning Gammon for ruining his and his family's life.

Gammon then looked at where Douglas his son was taken too. It was a now defunct care home called Edington Home for wayward children so the trail was cold unless the guy in the pub was Mickey Falham's son. John decided to go home get changed and wait for Saron to call.

SMILE

John had just come off the phone with
DCI Burns when Saron called.
"He is in John and I think he has been
drinking a fair bit". "Ok on my way
Saron".
It was a dreadful night, very cold with the
promise of more snow for the Peak
District. He arrived at the Tow'd Man but
as he parked up he realised if it was
Douglas Falham he would know him so
John called into the kitchen to ask Saron
for help. If he had been drinking he would
possibly open up to a beautiful girl. He
told Saron where he was taken, Edington
House, if he was the man.
Saron nipped upstairs and changed into
quite a revealing top. She wandered past
Falham.

"Hey sweetheart, you are looking gorgeous are you going to sit and have a Christmas drink with me?" That was the opening she wanted. Falham ordered them both drinks. "How long you worked here?"

"It's mine, well, mine and my business partner". "Oh wow, you look too young to own all this" he said in a creepy way.

"Must be good genes" she said.

"So Douglas, you are not from round these parts then?" "No, I lived down South for many years but I used to come walking up here and I did my Duke of Edinburgh award in the Peaks".

Saron saw an opportunity. "Was that through school?" Sensing Falham's unease she pushed on with the questioning.

Falham sensed something wasn't right and

SMILE

quickly changed the subject. "Enough of me are you from round these parts?" "Originally from Trissington". "Oh, never been there, saw something in the local papers about some dressing up of wells with clay and flower petals all seemed a bit Pagan to me". "Oh no, it was the way the villagers gave thanks for their water, you should see the village, it is very pretty". "Is there a pub there?" "Yes, the Wop and Take". "Why don't you take me one night this week? Just as a friend of course I mean, a pretty thing like you must have more suitors than a film star". Saron blushed, she thought Douglas was a bit creepy but he seemed nice and maybe if she got to know him he would open up with the information John needed. "Tell you what Douglas, let's go now, the village and the pub are lovely at this time of year".

Douglas smiled, they drank up and Saron told Donna she would be back around eleven. She forgot John was in the kitchen. John sat waiting for her, it was now almost 10.30pm, surely she had the information he needed by now. Donna came through. "What are you doing in the kitchen?" "It's a long story, more to the point, what is Saron mucking about at?" Oh, she left ages ago with that creepy guy, she said they were going to Trissington but she would be back about 11.00pm". "Shit, why did she do that?" "Is she in danger John?"

"I honestly don't know, did you hear any of their conversation Donna?" "Sorry, I have been too busy

SMILE

although I did hear him say he had done his Duke of Edinburgh award in the Peaks". "Donna I'm going back to the station, as soon as Saron gets back tell her to call me please". "Ok John will do". Gammon got back to the station much to the surprise of the front desk.

"Evening Sir". "Good evening Di". Gammon grabbed a coffee and headed to his office. He started to look for records for Duke of Edinburgh awards, sure enough he found Edington Home for wayward children and the first name was Douglas Falham, this was the man. Gammon could feel excitement welling up inside of him he called back to Donna. "Is Saron back yet?" "No John, she has a key though so I am locking up and going to bed, it's been a long day". "Just do me one last favour, see if Saron's car is on the car park". "Just a minute John". Donna was gone a short while and returned. "Yes, it looks like they went in his car John". "Ok, thanks Donna" "What's with the secrecy?" "I will tell you when I know more".

Gammon checked DVLA and police records, Douglas Falham had a speeding ticket on the 3rd December, his address was Wareham Farm Puddle Dale.

Gammon knew the farm, his dad had bought Gyp the collie dog from the people who owned the farm but he had heard they had emigrated to Spain and rented out the house and a couple of outbuildings but the land another farmer bought.

"Di, I want armed response and back up to Wareham Farm Puddle Dale, nobody is to

SMILE

do anything until I get there, please ensure
they understand that order Di". Gammon
knew if Falham had Saron there he would
kill her before he tried to escape and blue
flashing lights would tip him off.

Gammon got to the top of the drive just
before the rest arrived, he explained to
Sergeant Truman of the Rapid Response
team what he thought they might find,
Gammon was handed a bullet proof vest to
put on.

They stealthily headed to the two out
buildings, there was a light on in the larger
one and John could hear Saron. Why are
you doing this she kept saying. Gammon
gave the signal and they burst in from two
doors, Falham had a knife at Saron's
throat. "Drop the knife, we don't want to
shoot" said Truman. Falham just laughed

Gammon knew what he had to do because
Falham would kill Saron and laugh as he
got shot because he would have achieved
what his warped mind had told him.
Gammon lurched at Falham knocking
Saron to the floor, Falham struck Gammon
on the arm before Truman could get a
clear shot, Truman hit Falham in the
centre of the forehead killing him
immediately.

"You ok DI Gammon?" "Yeah, it's just a
nick, I will nip to Bixton and get it
dressed". They untied Saron, Gammon
wanted to shout at Saron for going with
Falham but, how could he? she looked so
pale and at least she was alive.

Gammon started looking round the barn,
he found Fleur's handbag. This was
definitely the killer, he had it wrong, all

SMILE

along it wasn't just a random guy who had it in for Gammon.

Saron and John went to the hospital before Saron did a statement. He had confessed it all. He said his father and mother committed suicide because Gammon hadn't prosecuted people who ripped him off. The reality was, it wasn't Gammon's decision not to follow up but he couldn't tell Mickey Falham at the time and now it had cost his sister her life and very nearly Saron's life.

Chapter 2

John could now bury his sister, it was her wish to be buried with her real father who was John's father, Uncle Graham.

The funeral was set for January 7th It was a bitter day as they arrived at St Helen's Church at Rowksly. There were only a handful of people, Saron and John, Donna, Heather Burns, DI Lee and DI Smarty came along to support John.

The vicar climbed the pulpit of the little church.

"Dearly beloved, we are here today to celebrate the life of Fleur Dubois a remarkable lady who served not just her own country but our country and several others. Although I never met Fleur her brother gave me an insight into the life and times of Fleur and she certainly packed in

SMILE

a lot in the years we were blessed to have her on this earth.

John has chosen some hymns and would like to say a few words also. If you would all stand and sing hymn number 313 in the green books, Morning has Broken". They all stood and the vicar did the bulk of the singing Saron gripped John's arm, she had never seen him this upset before. The hymn finished and the vicar gestured for John to come to the pulpit, he was clearly shaken as he started his eulogy

"First of all, thank you to everybody that have taken the time to come here today, most of you didn't know Fleur and maybe I didn't really know her. The job she did took all her time and one of the reasons none of her work colleagues are here today is for that special reason, they live in a very secretive world totally different than ours.

We both found each other later in our lives because of circumstances. My sister was bright, intelligent and above all loyal and I will miss her", John had to stop, a tear rolled down his cheek, he wiped it away and carried on. "I will miss her so very much, her death was so unnecessary, the man that killed her didn't know the full facts. I would like to say something that I have written". Donna and Saron were both crying.

"Little French butterfly, you are so special to me. You came into my life and gave me happiness, trust and loyalty and for that you will never be forgotten. When you arrive in heaven look down and smile

SMILE

knowing you made your brother very
happy to have had a sister like you."
John couldn't say anymore and returned to
Saron.

"Thank-you John, if you would like to
sing our next hymn, number 202 in the
green book, The day though gavest Lord is
ended, before we do, John has asked that
you join him at the Tow'd Man for
refreshments after the service, please
stand". They all stood and sang, as usual
the vicar had the loudest voice.

The coffin left the church to a Marvin
Gaye song, What's Going on? Saron left
John to carry the coffin and headed back
to the Tow'd man.

John arrived back about a half hour later
determined to drink himself into oblivion

at least to try and forget what Falham had done to him.

John arrived at the same time as Kev and Doreen. "Hey, come here lad, so sorry to hear about Fleur, just got a text from Shelley Etchings, we were coming up from Stansted after flying in from Egypt or we would have been back for you. Shelley said to tell you Jack hasn't been too good that's why they haven't come". "That's ok Doreen, I appreciate you both coming". "Very, very sorry lad" Kev said, putting a hand on John's shoulder. "Come on, let's have a drink and celebrate her life". "Good idea Saron". Saron wandered over to Doreen, "I have never seen him so upset, we will have to watch him Doreen". "Saron you are the only

SMILE

thing constant in his life, why don't you get back together?" "I do love him Doreen but he has got this self -destruct button and I don't want to go through that again". "It's such a shame, he is a lovely lad". "I know, just excuse me while I help Kathy and Donna get the food out".

Heather Burns was stood talking to DI Smarty and DI Lee when she took a call. "Ma'am, another body has been found at a Meaning Stone" said PC Magic. "Where Magic?" "On Toad Hole moor, I have sent DI Milton as he knows the area well having lived in Toad Holes for a long time Ma'am. "What about Forensics?" "Yes, they are on their way now". "Ok I will see them there shortly".

"Dave, Peter, you two stop here with John, don't tell him about this, he has got enough on today, I'll handle this and will see you tomorrow at a 9.00 am meeting when hopefully Wally has something to tell us". She quietly slipped away, John was too busy drinking to mind who was there and who wasn't.

Burns arrived at Toad Holes moor, she could see the white forensic tent blowing in the wind and DI Milton, DS Bass and DS Yap talking to a man and woman. "What we got Carl?" "This is Mr and Mrs Perry, they found the body". Mrs Perry looked shaken but Mr Perry seemed ok. When Burns started talking to him he told her he worked in a mortuary for twenty-seven years until he retired three years ago, they were on a walking holiday in the Peak District from Cambridge.

SMILE

"We had been told the night before by a local guy that there was a Meaning Stone on Toad Holes moor so we decided to have a walk up here not expecting to find this body propped up against it and his eyes replaced with dice showing the number one". "Thank you, Mr Perry, just let my officers take your details, how long will you be staying in the Peaks?" "About another two weeks DCI Burns, we are stopping at the Wobbly Man". "Just a thought, did you know the name of the guy who told you about the Meaning Stone?" "I think his name was Maurice but I'm not totally sure, Rick Hieb would know though". "Ok that's great thank you, if you think of anything else here is my number".

"DI Milton I am taking DS Bass with me, I've got a hunch about this Maurice guy who told them about the Meaning Stone".

"Ok Sir. "See you at the station tomorrow, tell Wally I want something by 9.00 am in the morning".

Heather and DS Bass drove down into the village to speak with Rick Hieb landlord at The Wobbly Man.

Rick said the guy wasn't a local but had been staying at the Wobbly Man for about six months, he said he was very secretive but paid on time every week but that he also came and went at funny hours of the day.

"Which room is his Mr Hieb?" "Room four, the en-suite room, it's our best room". "Is the guy in?" "No, he said he had to nip to London early this morning

SMILE

but would be back about 10.00 am in the morning, he was quite adamant he didn't want his room cleaned while he was away".

"Well I need to see it Mr Hieb". Rick took DS Bass and DCI burns up the stairs and along the corridor to room four. "I don't really like doing this, I mean, the guy has paid for his privacy". "Trust me we need to see inside that room".

Hieb opened the door and Burns said they would lock it when they had finished and bring the key to him. When they entered it seemed quite tidy and normal, Burns started going through the drawers while Bass checked under the bed. "Got a suitcase here Ma'am but its locked". "Force the lock Kate". "If we find something will it stand up in court?"

"It wasn't locked was it Kate?" For the
first time Kate could see how Burns had
climbed the ladder, she didn't always stick
to the rules.

Kate put the small case on the bed and
forced the lock, everything they ever
wanted was in the case, paper cuttings
about each murder, a chart naming the
victims and why they had to die, the
evidence was overwhelming. "Kate, I
think we have our killer, bring the case".
They locked the door behind them and
Burns had a word with Hieb, she told him
they would be arresting Maurice. "What's
his surname Mr Hieb?" "Let me look,
Seward, Maurice Seward". "Ok, you tell
nobody about this suitcase and I will have
officers waiting to arrest this man as soon
as he arrives, they will be here at 8.00am

SMILE

so will need letting in please". "Not a problem".

Burns and Bass headed back to Bixton to take a closer look at the suitcase and its contents.

There was everything documented, how he drugged his victims, how he terrified them and cut their eyes out before letting them bleed to death.

Confident she had her man she so wanted to let Gammon know but thought it best to call him in the morning.

By now Gammon was wrecked and Saron put him to bed, most people had left anyway. The following morning Burns called John, he had a head like Gateshead. Saron was sorting him some ibuprofen to take when he came downstairs, he hugged her and said, we have the killer Saron, it was like his headache and everything was gone. "Oh, great news John, are you ok to drive?" "Yes, I'm fine, I feel a bit woolly but I'll be ok. They got the murderer but he did kill again yesterday sadly on Toad Hole Moor. DCI Burns wanted me to be the arresting officer but her police work found the killer and right is right so I'll take the 9.00am meeting and she will arrest this man at 10.00am when he arrives at the Tow'd Man".

John drove to Bixton after thanking Saron, he said he would take her for a meal the following week as a thank you plus it might get them back together he thought. Wally had all the information on the victim, his name was Sammy Goldstein he was a jeweller from London, Gammon

SMILE

knew of him, he was bent as the day was long.

"He died from bleeding to death and was murdered where he was found, he also had traces of the paralysing drug called scopolamine or Devils Breath which appears to have been used on all the victims, it's from Columbia and it renders people to be paralysed and in some cases they will do whatever they are told which in this case would have meant walking to the Meaning Stone, that's how he got them to these remote places so easily. On the stone were these words

"To be first may mean to be last. To be last may mean to be first. You are on this journey of first and last take heed your journey may end"

There was the victims eyeball but only one. He bled to death where the stone is". "Ok, thank you Wally, so you all know DCI Burns did some cracking police work with DS Bass, they found a suitcase with all the information needed to arrest a Maurice Seward from London who has been staying at the Wobbly Man pub for some six months while he carried out his gruesome murders, we should know quite soon why. Thank you everybody for your hard work and commitment and to the officers that spent their Christmas watching Harry Salt who it seems had nothing to do with the case, a big thank you".

Burns and Bass came back with Seward and DCI Burns asked Gammon to come in with her, she said Seward seemed over

SMILE

confident and he had a local lawyer who he called.

They assembled in interview room two and DS Bass started the recording by introducing everybody.

"So Mr Seward or can I call you Maurice?" "Maurice is fine" he replied. Seward was about six feet tall with a short -cropped hair cut, the type you would see in the films about the 1920's gangsters. He was well dressed in a black suit and polished black shoes.

"Before we go any further my client would like to make a complaint that his room at the Wobbly Man public house in Toad Holes was searched without his knowledge or his approval I want that put on the record".

"Mr Guy, your client was staying at the Wobbly Man public house and the landlord and owner of the establishment opened the room and gave us permission to search it so everything was done legally". "DI Gammon I disagree, the suitcase found under the bed apparently was forcibly opened by one of your officers". Heather Burns dived in "for the record, DS Bass, who is recording this conversation, found the suitcase and put it on the bed, the lock was not forced by either myself or DS Bass, isn't that correct DS Bass?" "Yes Ma'am, the suitcase was already open". "Bollocks" Seward countered. "That was bloody forced open". "For the tape Mr Seward, that is your word against two serving police officers and I am sure after this interview

SMILE

any court in the land would believe two serving officers against a murderer". "Mr Gammon my client cannot be spoken too like that". "Oh really? I'm sorry, I meant to say a murdering scumbag!!" "So Maurice, is this your suitcase?" Gammon showed him the suitcase DS Bass had found. "No comment". "Are the contents in here yours?" "No comment". Gammon then showed him his signature in the Wobbly Man sign in book. "This is your writing correct?". "Yes" he replied all belligerent. "So, would we all agree that the writing here about the murders and the sample of the writing I showed you are one of and the same?" "No comment".

Next Gammon showed him his phone. "Is this your phone?" "Yes" he replied. "You see Mr Seward, today's fancy phones have GPS built in so we had our tech people look at it and it pretty much put you at the scene of all these murders now is that a coincidence?" "No comment" Seward said but he now wasn't as confident.

"Maurice, you must realise that I have enough in this suitcase to charge you, I would suggest you cooperate and we can say you were helpful in our enquiries which will help you in your case". Seward's solicitor leaned forward and spoke with Seward. "May we take a few minutes please DI Gammon?" "Of course" DS Bass said that a break was required from the questioning. Gammon DCI Burns and DS Bass left the room leaving Seward with his solicitor.

SMILE

They gave him ten minutes then returned. DS Bass started the tape again.

"So Maurice, what's it to be?" "My client will cooperate fully DI Gammon".

"Ok, let's start again Maurice. Are you the person responsible for the six murders where each victim's eyes were removed and dice used to replace them?" "Yes".

"Speak up please Maurice for the tape". "Yes, I killed those people". "Can you explain what the significance of The Meaning Stones was?" "No significance, I used them purely to throw you off the scent, each murder was planned because of who they were". "Explain more Maurice".

"This goes back twelve years, I was the owner of a club in Soho, business was good until one-night Gary Birch came into

my club with Leslie Brough, I didn't know
them, I was in the back when my manager
came and said two guys were buying loads
of people in the club drinks, nothing
wrong with that you could say but they
would not pay, my manager came to tell
me so I went out to confront them. Birch
hit me so hard I thought he had broken my
skull, he said from now on he would bring
friends to my club at my expense.
Brough hadn't said anything at this point
but over the next months he was as bad as
Birch, if not worse. One night a man came
into the club asking for me, his name was
Filigree Matkin, he had a woman with
him, her name was Marilyn Wilson he said
they had come to buy the club but I could
stop and run it as the manager. I asked
who wanted to buy it and he said Johnny

SMILE

Lomax I then asked what he was offering he laughed at me, how does a pound sound? I thought he was joking but he wasn't, over the next few months I had hassle from police and everybody involved with Lomax. After almost a year I signed my club over to Lomax, he then told me that Robert Bloom would help me run the club. Over the next couple of years, I began to hate Bloom in fact I hated all of them involved.

It was two years after my club was taken off me that my life took its final downturn, I was arrested on a charge of robbing a jewellers, the jeweller was Sammy Goldsmiths and he said I held him up by gunpoint although no gun was ever found because I didn't do it, it was all a set up.

I got ten years and it was while I was in Bristol prison that I planned my revenge, I read about you Mr Gammon and a case you had solved. I decided to kill these six people but to make it look like a serial killer hence the dice and the Meaning Stones. My one mistake was with that couple, I had a few drinks one night and they were talking about walks and the Meaning Stones. If I hadn't have opened my mouth I would have been home and dry because they were the only people I wanted dead".

"Maurice Seward I am charging you with kidnapping, use of a paralysis drug and the eventual mutilation and death of Leslie Brough also known as Anthony Smidge, Robert Bloom, Marilyn Wilson, Filigree Columbus Shakespeare Matkin, Gary

SMILE

Birch and Sammy Goldstein. Take him to the holding cells please DS Bass".

They all left leaving Gammon with his head in hands an DCI Burns looking on. "Are you ok John?" "Sorry Heather, yes, it's been a hard few days, well done, that was cracking police work Heather".

"Thanks John, I suppose I'd better arrange a celebration at the Spinning Jenny tomorrow night". "You'd best Heather" John said and smiled.

The station was jubilant that they had their killer, it had been a hell of a ride, first they lost a colleague in Danny Kiernan then John' sister falls prey to a scumbag from years back then the six murders now solved. The team were in a celebratory mood but John still felt cheated that he had lost his sister.

That night they all headed to the Spinning Jenny, Wez and Lindsay had put a great spread on for the team. By 9.15pm though there was only John, Carl, Kate, Tom and Martin left and the new boys were only really stopping because John Gammon was there.

"Ok who's for a brandy a piece?" DS Kate Bass was the first with a glass. DI Tom Stampfer thought he could see an opportunity with the pretty Kate Bass so he wandered over. "We haven't really got to know each other have we Kate?" "Guess not". "So, are you seeing anybody?" "Yes, I can see a lot of people in here tonight Tom" she said sarcastically. "No, you know what I mean". "Tom if this is some kind of drunken chat up line, try it when you are

SMILE

sober" and she wandered off to talk with John and Martin.

"Chancing his arm was he Kate?" "Just a little bit Sir". "Well I can't blame him, you are a pretty girl". Kate blushed. "Thank you, come on, brandies all round". By now Wez the landlord had joined them and John remembered how ill he felt after drinking Brandy with Wez the last time so he decided to call it a night.

On the way home he got a text from Saron, "come up and see me tomorrow night I have something for you". Wow John thought, that certainly cheered him up so he replied "Ok", he didn't want sound too keen.

Chapter 3

The following day John arrived at Bixton, PC Magic said DI Smarty said to let him know he was talking with a couple from Dilley Dale. "What about Magic?". "I don't know sir, he was covering me on the desk while I nipped to the loo and when I came back he was just going into interview room one with this couple".

"Ok, thanks Magic".

John entered the room not sure what to expect. Smarty was sat opposite a couple aged maybe in their mid -thirties, both well- dressed, a bit like two Marks and Spencer's dummies John thought.

"Oh, this is DI Gammon, this is Mr Graham Much and his wife Lorna John".

"Pleased to meet you both, what appears

SMILE

to be the problem Dave?" "I'll let Graham
tell you".

"It's our daughter Chelsea, she is eighteen
well, nineteen in a couple of weeks, she is
a hairdresser at Cut and Blow in Dilley
Dale, that's where we live Mr Gammon.
Since she was a little girl she dreamed
about being a model". They showed John
a picture of pretty auburn- haired girl.
Thinking this was taking some time John
tried to hurry them along.

"So, what is the problem Graham?"

"My wife took a phone call the other night
about 9.00pm, it was a man, he said he
was calling Chelsea about the modelling
she had applied for, we didn't know
anything about it but my wife took his
number". They showed Gammon the
number and DI Smarty wrote it down.

"When Chelsea came in, it would be about 10.40pm because the local news had just finished on ITV, I like to keep up with local events". John was thinking, get on with it man.

"We told Chelsea what the man had said and my wife questioned her, she got quite angry with Lorna saying what she did was none of her business and that we were a pair of boring old farts with no ambition in life. Lorna was quite upset as Chelsea stormed off to her room. Lorna had gone to bed and I was watching Question Time, I do like to hear those people debate, everyone should have a voice hey Mr Gammon?" Gammon was at this point thinking he wished Graham Much hadn't.

"Anyway, Anna Sowerby, you know the lady that used to be on TV and is now an

SMILE

MP? she was talking when I heard the front door go so I got up to see what was happening and I saw our Chelsea get in a red car, I think I caught a glimpse of a man in the driving seat but I wasn't sure and the car sped off, we live in a quiet cul-de- sac so I'm not sure what the next Neighbourhood watch are going to say".
"Tell Mr Gammon about her not coming home Graham, that's why we are here". "I was getting to that bit Lorna, yes, Chelsea hasn't been home since and we are worried".
"Mr Much please don't think I am being disrespectful but the police use fourteen percent of their resources looking for reported missing people and a good number of those missing turn up after forty-eight hours. What I suggest is, if

Chelsea hasn't returned in forty-eight hours call me on this number" and Gammon handed Graham Much his card. "Then if she is still missing we will start looking in more depth".

"I thought the police would have helped us more than this Mr Gammon". "
I understand your misgivings Mrs Much but we only have a certain amount of resources", with that Gammon left the room.

Oh, that was painful he thought. She has most probably phoned her boyfriend to say she had an argument with her parents and she is making them suffer for a bit which is often the case with teenage runaways, Gammon went back to his office, Heather looked a bit ropey from the night before but she said she had quite a few plaudits

SMILE

for solving the case. John was quite impressed with Heather, she didn't want the credit unlike most of the DCI's he had the pleasure to work with.

"Isn't it nice to just have day to day policing for a change John?" "I suppose the next thing will be Seward court case, I have just had a man and his wife come into the station to report their eighteen well, almost nineteen-year-old daughter missing. Usual stuff, daughter fell out with them last night and it sounds like her boyfriend picked her up. Her father went right around the houses in this monotone voice, to be honest I couldn't wait to get out of there". "Well at least you can smile John".

He decided to work his way through his paperwork, the usual task from hell he thought, the good thing was Saron had asked him to call for a present she had for him.

It was 6.00pm when he finally finished his last report. It was still quite cold outside and his windscreen was frozen up, John set about it with some de-icer. He arrived at the Tow'd Man and Saron said she was having the night off, she was sat at the bar talking to Kathy, she had some skinny light blue jean leggings with a cashmere dark blue jumper and a dark blue pair of kitten heel shoes, this girl just knew how to dress he thought.

"Hey John, how are you?" "Yeah good thanks, you are looking gorgeous". "Well thank you kind sir, get John a pint of Witches brew please Kathy". "I'm sure you are thinking that's quite apt" and she

SMILE

laughed showing a set of pearly white
teeth.

They sat talking and John was waiting for
his surprise to be revealed, Saron wasn't
letting on. Eventually John had to ask.

"Go on then what's my surprise?" "You
will have to come with me". This can't get
much better John thought. Saron took him
into her small living room, in a basket in
the corner was a white kitten. "Meet Dark
Chocolate John". "This is the surprise?"
"Don't be mad at me, you need something
to come home to at night John".

"Well it's not quite what I was expecting".
"What were you expecting Mr Gammon?"
and Saron threw her arms round his
shoulders, she kissed him passionately,
John soon returned the compliment.

It all felt so good as he kissed every inch of her porcelain like skin, she writhed in ecstasy as John worked his way from her neck all the way down her body.

He held her tight, she was the only thing he wanted in his life, for the first time since Fleur died he felt he had something, somebody who cared for him. They were breathless as they made love, after it was all over she laid her head on him, twirling the hairs on his chest. "John, you know I love you". "Can we be together then?"

"I don't know, you hurt me so bad John, I have to find a way of trusting you again then, maybe, but don't rush me please".

John felt ecstatic, this was all he wanted. The following morning John woke, he could smell bacon cooking, Saron was in the kitchen in his shirt and those little

SMILE

kitten heels and nothing else cooking. John grabbed her from behind kissing her neck. "Stop it Gammon if you want a bacon sandwich". "Ok, have I time for a shower?" "Hurry up then". John dashed upstairs showered and changed for work. Saron had done him his favourite bacon doorstep sandwich. "What am I going to do with DC?" "DC?" "Yeah, Dark Chocolate, I'm at work all day". "Roger Glazeback will put you a cat flap in your door if you ask him".

John left Saron and headed home with DC. He spoke with Roger, he said he would sort it out. John gave him some money for the cat flap and cat food and a drink for sorting then headed off for work.

For the first time in a long time he felt good about himself but he knew he couldn't force Saron, it had to be on her terms.

"Morning Sir". "Good morning Magic".
"DI Lee has Mr and Mrs Much in interview room one". "Oh no, not sure I can handle another ten minutes with that man, Ok, I'd best go in".

Gammon entered the room. "Good morning Mr and Mrs Much". They booth looked shaken. "What is it?" Mr Much passed his phone to Gammon. "I got this from our daughter" it was a short video, she didn't speak until it appeared somebody knocked the phone out of her hand. She was tied to a chair, clearly she was upset, her mascara running down her face from the tears.

"Mr much can I take your phone? our people might be able to trace the call".

SMILE

"She is being held against her will Mr
Gammon". "Peter get this phone to the IT
lads quick, time maybe of the essence". DI
Lee left the room with the phone.
"Mr Much, the car you said you saw on
the night your daughter left, did you see
the number plate?" "No, it was dark but I
think it was a Peugeot 206, red, a guy I
work with has got a black one same
shape".
"Look, we will get your daughter back,
whoever is holding her has made some
serious mistakes". "Please Mr Gammon,
she is my little girl, we only managed to
have Chelsea through IVF and could not
afford anymore, she is all we have".
DI Lee came back in and whispered
something in Gammon's ear. "Ok, look,
go home, we have a lead and will be in

touch". "Thank- you Mr Gammon". They left, DI Lee had told Gammon that the signal was from a disused mill in Rowksly, he said he had arranged armed response but they were not to do anything until you get there John. "Great Peter, well done".

Gammon and Lee set off for Rowksly and the disused flour mill. "Wasn't this owned by Bagshaw's until it closed?" "Yes, I think so John, I think it ran until about 1977, there was talk of it being turned into luxury flats but there is a lot of hostility from Peak Park planning, it's been going on for years so it's just fallen into decay". At the top of the drive that lead to Bagshaw's flour mill there were three police vans with seven armed response personnel, "Ok lads, I can see a white van

SMILE

down there but no red Peugeot, let's just take it steady". Gammon and Lee were handed vests to wear. The mill was deathly quiet then DI Lee pointed to the South facing area and whispered he had heard voices. "Ok, go on in lads". Armed response burst in shouting, "hit the floor" to a couple by the window, they looked petrified as they did as instructed. Two of the officer's hand- cuffed them before picking them up off the ground. "Names" the officer barked. The guy said Richie Sparks and the girl said Helena Worth. Gammon looked at DI Lee, wrong people. "What are you doing here?" The girl looked sheepish. "I'll ask again, what are you doing here?" Eventually Sparks said he and Helena had started an affair and this was the first time they had met, they worked together at the bakery in Rowksly. "My husband won't find out will he?" Gammon intervened. "No, but I suggest you keep away from here. You say you haven't been here before?" they both said no. "So, you won't have seen this girl" and he showed them a picture of Chelsea. "No, never seen her but like I said, we have never been here before". "Ok release them, just don't come back".

Well that was a waste of time, John. Gammon told the armed response they could leave and he and DI Lee would take a look around.

"Hey Peter, I think this is the room the girl was in". "Shall I get Wally here John?" "No point looking at it, whoever has got this poor girl is well gone., let's go and see Mr and Mrs Much and see if we can take a

SMILE

look in Chelsea's bedroom, we might come across something".

DI Gammon and DI Lee headed for Dilley Dale and the address Magic gave them, Number three Christie View, a quiet cul-de-sac of five four-bedroom detached houses.

Gammon rang the door-bell which played I am Sailing by Rod Stewart. "That's novel John". Gammon just smiled at DI Lee. Lorna Much came to the door. "Oh Mr Gammon have you found her?" "May we come in?" Lorna showed them to the living room which was tastefully decorated. "I'm afraid whoever is holding your daughter moved on before we could locate them. Could we possibly take a look around Chelsea's bedroom?" "Yes, by all means, I'm afraid Graham is at work, he decided to go back to take his mind off it, he is a Bricklayer in Ackbourne". They climbed the stairs and Lorna showed them her daughter's room.

It was like all teenage girls' rooms, full of posters of their favourite pop stars, Chelsea also had framed magazine covers of models. They started to look in the draws. "Hey John, got something here". "What is it?". "It's a business card for a model agency". "Let me look Pete". It was a white business card with the name of the agency, "IN THE BUFF" Model Agency. Contact Sandra Cullen and a phone number. "Ok, put that in your pocket, let's carry on" there was a photo album and almost all of the pictures were of Chelsea and two other girls. Gammon took it

SMILE

downstairs and asked Lorna who the other two girls were.

"Oh, they are Chelsea's best friends that girl with dark hair Is Kerry Vaney from Dilley Dale and the blond girls is Lizzie Tuffs from Rowksly". "Could you give my colleague their address's please Lorna?".

DI Lee took the details. "We will be in touch Lorna". "Please get her back Mr Gammon". "We will Lorna". They left poor Lorna and decided to go to the model agency to speak with Sandra Cullen. They rang the number and Cullen answered, she said she would be in the office for about another two hours interviewing and what was it about. Gammon said he preferred to talk face to

face so they headed for "In the Buff" at
Ackbourne High Street.

"In the Buff" was above Daltons betting
office on Ackbourne High Street.
Gammon showed the young girl their
warrant cards and asked to speak to
Sandra Cullen. "Please take a seat". She
went off and after about five minutes a tall
blonde-haired woman in her mid- thirties
introduced herself as Mary Cullen, "please
come into my office".

The office was adorned with pictures of
models both men and women. "Right, how
can I help you?" "May I call you Sandra?"
"By all means". "Ok Sandra, we are
looking for a missing person well, actually
this girl, Chelsea Much" and he pushed a
photograph of Chelsea towards Cullen.
"Do you know the girl?" "I can't say I do

SMILE

but I have hundreds of wanna be's come
through that door so she could have been
to see me but I don't honestly know".
"Would you not have any records
Sandra?"
"Look, kids come here believing they have
what it takes, some of them are barely
fifteen but they say they are twenty and
they give you a false address and name,
we take their picture, if we think they have
a chance we recommend a portfolio of
pictures which they pay for and we use to
tout round the agencies and magazines".
"Ok, I understand, so what if a girl goes
through all that and you get her a spot at,
let's say GQ magazine. Do they not want
ID?" "Look Mr Gammon, at that point it's
not my problem, we make the money on
the portfolio, if, as you say, GQ took this

imaginary girl on, they would do the background check and if she is legal we then get 10% of any payments made to the model we find for three years, a contract which they sign at the time of the Portfolio shoot".

"Nice little business model Sandra with no risk hey? Had any success's?" "Yes a few, Annabella Fielding otherwise known as Cherry Lucan, she has been on most of the front pages of the best magazines, also Brandon Rike, he just won a big modelling contract for Dalesman Catalogues and shops so yes, we make a good living". Well if you do hear of Chelsea be sure to get in touch Sandra". "Will do gents" and she showed Gammon and Lee out.

"Let's call it a night Peter and we can go and see Chelsea's friends tomorrow".

SMILE

It was almost 5.45pm when they got back
to Bixton station, Gammon dropped DI
Lee off and called DCI Burns on the way
up to get her up to speed Maurice Seward
was due in court in three weeks and they
would possibly need to be there as
witness's. After the conversation John
decided to call in at the Spinning Jenny on
the way home hopeful Lindsay would do
him a take out.

The pub was quite busy and John was
surprised to see Sheba with Carol Lestar,
Shelly Etchings, Tracey Rodgers and
Cheryl. "Evening ladies, what are you lot
celebrating?" "Carol and Jimmy's
engagement". "Oh right, let me get a
couple of bottles of bubbly for you,
congratulations Carol". "Thank you John,
we are having a party at the Wobbly Man

on Saturday, you are of course invited and bring a lucky girl". Sheba looked across at John, John winked.

He left the girls to it and stood at the bar talking to Wez. "Will Lindsay do me a take away?" "I would think so, what would you like?" "Can I have the tagine with rice mate?" "Blimey John, I was just going to say, Lindsay made it today and I was test pilot, absolutely gorgeous mate, great choice". Wez went off to tell Lindsay, Sheba saw her opportunity. "You ok John?" "Yes, sorry I haven't been in touch, work and all that you know." "No problem, are you coming to Jimmy and Carol's engagement on Saturday?" Yes, and I will pick you up if you want". "Well we only have to come here, Wez and Lindsay have organised a bus from here at

SMILE

7.00pm to the Wobbly Man and back".
"Ok, I'll pick you up at 6.30pm then".
"Ok, look I'd best get back to the crowd".
"Ok, see you Saturday". Sheba left and
Lindsay came through with the tagine.
"Hope its ok John, I've only ever made it
for the family, never done it
commercially". "It will be fine I'm sure,
right there you go Wez" John paid his bill
and said goodnight.

John remembered about the kitten, DC,
and wondered if Roger had the cat flap
sorted. As he pulled up at the cottage he
could see a pair of eyes peering from the
cat flap, little DC was waiting for him. He
opened the door and DC was around his
legs in a flash. Roger had done a good job
of the cat flap and he had bought plenty of
cat food and a couple of bowls. John ate

his dinner then poured himself a large Jameson's and sat on his settee with a book, DC was straight there curled up on his lap. John had to admit to himself that it felt quite nice to have something greet him when he came home, as usual, Saron knew what she was doing he thought.

The following morning, he showered and got ready for work stroking DC as he left, back in a bit mate he said smiling to himself that he was talking to a cat like his Mum used to.

He arrived at Bixton and told DS Bass that she was going with him too see the friends of Chelsea Much. "Get the addresses Kate and let's go and shake the tree, let's go to Keri Vaney's house first". "Ok Sir, that's Crowstones House at Dilley Dale". "Yes, I

SMILE

know where that is Kate, it's just off the main road across from newsagents". They arrived at Crowstones House and knocked on the green and cream painted door, an elderly lady answered, Gammon and Bass showed their warrant cards. "Do come in" she said, "it's too cold to be stood out there Mr Gammon". "Are you Mrs Vaney?" "Oh no, I'm Monica James, my daughter was killed in a car crash with her husband Gordon Vaney". "Oh, I am sorry only this is the address that we were given for a Miss Keri Vaney". "Yes, that's correct, Keri is my granddaughter, she has lived with me since Gordon and Julie passed away".

"We are investigating a missing person and we believe Keri was a good friend and would like to ask her a few questions".

"Well if you find her let me know please
Mr Gammon, you see Keri was only
twelve when her parents died and she took
it badly, I tried to be a parent to her but
she resented it, to be honest Mr Gammon
she left the house three days ago and she
hasn't been back, she did take some
clothes but there are still some here. I had
nipped for my pension and when I got
back she was gone. It's perhaps for the
best, she is almost twenty and I can't be
doing with that loud music all the time.
I'm sure she will contact me Mr
Gammon". "Well when she does, please
call me". Gammon handed Monica James
his card and they left.

"There is something not right here Kate
and I think that model agency is the key,

SMILE

let's go and see Lizzie Tuffs in Rowksly
on the way back to the Station".
They found Number four Stinton Terrace
in Rowksly, they were a row of railway
cottages still painted in British Rail red
with cream coloured doors and windows.
Gammon knocked on the door and a pretty
girl maybe twenty hears old answered. "DI
Gammon and DS Bass" and they showed
their warrant cards. "Are you Lizzie
Tuffs?" "Yes, I am, what is this about?"
"May we come in?" "Oh, ok" she showed
them into the kitchen which was in quite a
chaotic state with a sink full of pots and
bread crumbs all over the working side.
"This is my boyfriend Craig". The guy
stood up and said good morning, Gammon
picked up that he had quite a posh accent.
"We live together Mr Gammon".

"We wondered if you could help us, we are looking for Chelsea Much and potentially a young lady called Keri Varney, we believe they are friends of yours". "I am a good friend of Chelsea but Keri is a bit of a loose cannon so I try to avoid her as much as I can".

"When was the last time you saw Chelsea?" "It would have been about a week ago". "Did she say she was going away or anything?" "No, oh no, wait a minute, she did say she had got a modelling job in Tenerife I think, she said it's for an eighteen to thirty holiday brochure".

"Which agency gave her the work?" "The one we are all with, "In the Buff" it was actually Keri Varney that got us involved". "So, have you done some

SMILE

modelling jobs then Lizzie?" "Yes, I've done two, they are very good, all expenses paid and they pay your fee straight into the bank, I got five hundred and fifty pounds for a shoot for Thimbles Clothing didn't I Craig?" Craig nodded. "So, Sandra Cullen got you the work?" "Well, her company did, I don't know if Sandra actually got it for me".

"So, getting back to Chelsea, you haven't spoken for a week?" "That's correct". "Ok Lizzie well thank you for your time, it is possible that her parents are over reacting". "Yes, Lorna and Graham are very old fashioned, she was always complaining about how they never support her". "Parent's hey Lizzie? Thanks for your time". Craig the boyfriend got up and shook John's hand again and they left.

"Looks like a case of over powering parents hey sir?" "Possibly Kate but we always have to investigate" Gammon said in a dismissive tone.

"When you get back start a full search on the model agency and in particular the owners". "Will do sir".

They arrived back at Bixton and DCI Burns called John into her office. "This is Pearson Dalby the prosecutor in the Maurice Seward murder trial John". Dalby was a small balding man with half rimmed glasses and he wore a striped business suit. "How can I help?" "Well DI Gammon, you will be called as a witness at Maurice Seward's trial, he is claiming that he is insane!" "Well he is certainly that" and John laughed, Dalby never showed any emotion. "We don't want him going into a

SMILE

secure mental hospital we want life in a high security prison DI Gammon". "Sorry, I didn't mean to be flippant". "The case may rest on your assumption of the man, do I make myself clear?" "If you mean clear I will be honest and truthful in the witness box". "Then that will have to do Mr Gammon, thank you". Dalby dismissed Gammon like some naughty schoolboy, he obviously was implying he wanted Gammon to stretch the truth and Gammon wasn't about to do that. Gammon returned to his office grabbing a coffee on the way. He stood thinking about the Chelsea Much case. He was convinced there was more to this than just a missing person. It was an awful day, Losehill was barely visible from his office window, the rain lashed down his window pane, droplets racing to be first down the window pane to the sill.

Gammon decided to get his paperwork put away so he sat down, after almost four hours DS Bass came back into his office. "Not finding anything wrong with the modelling agency sir, Sandra Cullen appears to have two failed businesses behind her but no money concerns, she set the company up eight years ago with a the board of Directors which are Clive Winch, Alan Rose, Raznak Bolan and company secretary Aileen Stope. I am working on these characters next". "Ok, keep at it Kate, I have a feeling on this". "Will do sir". Gammon called it a night and left Bixton station, he noticed a missed call from Sheba, John called her back. "Hey how are you John?" "Good thanks". "It

SMILE

was just about Saturday's engagement party". "Oh blimey, sorry Sheba, I've been that busy at work it totally went out of my mind, shall I pick you up at 6.00pm then you said there is a bus Lindsay and Wez had set up to take us to the Wobbly Man is that correct?". "Yes John". "Ok, I'll pick you up at 6.00pm"

Here I go again he thought, just trying to sort Saron and I have every intention of spending the night with Sheba after the party.

John arrived at the Spinning Jenny, Tracey Rodgers was working the bar and Lindsay was sat having a drink and talking to her with Wez cooking in the kitchen, the pub was quite full. "Evening Lindsay". "Hello John, that's funny, we were just talking about you". "Hope it was nice?" "Well, because you caught that maniac that was killing all those people and tying them to the Meaning Stones we now have full accommodation again so the Pedigree I'm assuming you are about to order is on me!".

"Hello John, there you go, one pint of Pedigree. How are you tonight?" "Yeah good thanks Tracey what about you?" "How's Steve?" "Hardly seen him, he moved in with India about two week ago, they both seem loved up". "Well at least they are happy hey?". "I suppose so but it does seem a bit weird". "Steve has never been conventional Tracey trust me". She went off to serve somebody else. "So, John, you going to Caz and Jimmy's engagement party?" "Yes, I think Sheba booked us on the bus". "Sheba Filey?"

SMILE

"Yeah". "Oh yeah, she booked two places with Wez but I didn't know who she was going with, very pretty girl you have there John". John blushed and Lindsay, realising she was embarrassing him, quickly changed the subject.

"Do you think Wez will do me a take out?" "Sure he will John, what do you fancy?" "I think I'll just have the Croates pork sausages with glazed honey carrots; garden peas and Swinster mash, can I have the onion gravy in a pot separate please Lindsay?" "Well that's a nice easy one for him, he doesn't cook very often but he said to get Tracey in for the bar and told me to have a night off from the kitchen, that he would cover. It was just so hectic leading up to Christmas John and now we are starting to get into the camping season and they say that it's mental then". "Oh yeah, now that will be busy Lindsay". There wasn't anybody else in that John knew so he had one more pint and took his take away home.

DC was waiting as soon as John came through the door, she was all fussy around his legs, it was nice he thought, to have that bit of company. He poured himself a large Jameson's and sat and ate his dinner, it was a bit awkward as DC had decided to sit on his lap while he was eating.

SMILE

Chapter 4

The following morning John drove into work, he took the long route as he was quite early. This route took him down Dumpling Dale before climbing back onto the main Bixton road, climbing out of Dumpling Dale John remembered his Mum saying her grandma had said its actual name was Bixton Drop Dale but all the locals called it Dumpling Dale because of the tremendous rock formation on both sides of the ascent to Bixton road. Gammon arrived at Bixton to a sheepish PC Magic on the front desk. "I have Mr and Mrs Much in Interview room one, they were here at 7.30am, they said they want to talk to you". "Oh great, that's all I need to start my day Magic, did you give them a drink?" "Mrs Much didn't want

one and Mr Much insisted on Bixton
spring water, he said he drank nothing
else". "That figures Magic, grab me a
coffee mate, I think I am going to need it".
John entered the room, "Good morning Mr
and Mrs Much how can I help you?"
"Well it's like this Mr Gammon, me and
Lorna got to thinking last night, on the TV
they have that Crime Watch thing and
another program about missing persons,
we wondered if you think we should
contact them?"
"Graham, please don't think we aren't
taking this seriously but your daughter
hasn't been gone long in the grand scheme
of things, the phone incident could be just
a fall out with her boyfriend. We are
investigating her disappearance but you
also need to understand she is an adult and

SMILE

she also has rights. If we find her she can simply tell us to leave her alone and we are not allowed to discuss where she is with you, I'm sorry if this sounds harsh but that is the reality Graham".

"But it wouldn't hurt to get her name out there with all this social media. I said to Lorna I had to look up what social media was and it's that Twotter thing and Factbook isn't it?". "You mean Twitter and Facebook Graham?" "Yes, it's something like that Mr Gammon. I mean, I know young ones of today don't listen to their parents as much as maybe we did but we are good parents and our Chelsea knew that. Did I tell you I called her after my football team Mr Gammon?" "No, you didn't Graham". "Oh, I was fanatical wasn't I Lorna?" "Yes, he never missed a match home or away when we lived down London". John thought he should perhaps join in a bit. "What brought you up here Graham?" "It was Lorna's job, she is a nurse and her eldest sister lived up here and she used to come and stay with her and loved it so eventually she applied at Ackbourne Hospital and got accepted. I was a brickie so could get a job anywhere I guess, I work at Hayles Construction also in Ackbourne".

"Look Graham, Lorna, we are doing everything to find your daughter, my concern would be whoever has her and for whatever reasons may panic if the media get hold of it, those boys are only interested in the story not the outcome, you have to trust me on this Graham".

"We do Mr Gammon, I have been reading

SMILE

up on your career haven't I Lorna?" Lorna Much just nodded her head in agreement. "You are a very famous detective Mr Gammon and we do trust you, we just wondered what you thought, I hope you don't mind". "Not at all" Gammon said being very diplomatic when he actually just wanted to be left alone to solve the case.

"Ok Graham, Lorna, we will be in touch". "Thank you Mr Gammon" Lorna said. "Bet you can't remember Webby can you?" "Sorry Graham, Webby?" "David Webb, he was like you, a hundred percent always wanted to win didn't he Lorna?" "So you say Graham, come on let's let Mr Gammon get on".

"If I think of anything DI Gammon I will be in touch". "Thank you Graham". I bet he flippin will he said to himself. Gammon climbed the stairs to his office grabbing a dishwater coffee as he called it on the way.

John had just started his paperwork when DCI Burns came in. "What are we doing about the trial? we are expecting to be in court for three days" "There is a nice Hampton Inn close to the court, book us in there Heather". "Ok, I just wondered, I've not done a big case like this John and I am quite nervous". "It's a breeze Heather, you will be fine". In his mind he knew that wasn't the case when he and the team had cocked up on the Alison case a couple of year back.

With it now being Friday night and John seeing Saron for Jimmy and Carol's engagement party he decided to go home

SMILE

to DC. John picked fish and chips from
Annie's in Swinster and a fish for DC.
Annie's was a unique chip shop, she
cooked everything from her kitchen
serving it through a sliding window,
people queued in the back yard of her
terraced house. You had a choice, fish and
chips or fish, chips and mushy peas, none
of this curry or kebab stuff at Annie's. She
must have been almost eighty, Phil often
used to take him and Adam after hay
making as a treat and she must have been
in her sixties then he thought.
Armed with supper and little DC's as well
he arrived at the cottage. DC was waiting
as usual so John put her dinner down first.
He washed his hands and plated his dinner
out. DC didn't seem to be bothered about
her fish which John couldn't understand as

his was beautiful. The cat jumped on John's knee and started paddling through his trousers before settling down, he called it a night and DC followed.

The following morning, it being a Saturday, he decided to do some walking. He left the cottage at 9.00 am and for once headed down into Hittington. He climbed out of Hittington towards Dick Turpin's barn so called because it was alleged that Dick Turpin, the famous highway man, held up there one night after one of his daring raids. At the barn John poured himself a coffee from his flask and read what the plaque said on the barn commemorating Turpin.

From the barn he headed out towards the Staffordshire Derbyshire border and a little village called Knackerall, nobody

SMILE

knew how it got its name but it was certainly a village frozen in time. It had bakers, butchers, pub, school and an amazing church, it only needed a candlestick maker John thought. As he walked through the village he sensed the people were odd. His Mum said the village was always cut off during bad winters and she said they were all inter-breeds, she was probably right John thought. He decided not to stop, it just didn't feel comfortable, people were staring like he was from another planet!!

Leaving Knackerall he headed down the street towards Ropesmoor. Ropesmoor was a small hamlet but it surprisingly still had a pub, The Barrel. John decided to stop for a bit of lunch, what a mistake that was. Cole the landlord who was about

forty with blonde hair and always wore
shorts, summer or winter, insisted on John
trying Ropesmoor Treacle with his
Ploughman's, what he didn't tell John was
that the beer was seventeen percent proof,
illegal, and Cole brewed it in a shed at the
back of the pub.

John being John had two pints and could
feel the room swirling so he got Cole to
get him a taxi home to sleep it off. He set
his alarm for 5.15pm, that way if he still
felt iffy he could get Sheba to pick him up.
He fell in a deep sleep with DC insisting
on lying across his legs. at5.15pm the
alarm woke him, John decided to ring
Sheba just to be safe. She was fine like she
always was and said she would pick him
up at 6.30pm.

SMILE

Phyllis Swan had ironed some shirts so he had quite a choice, he wasn't sure what he would do if she called it a day. John wore his dark blue John Rocha jacket with a pair of light coloured Armani jeans and a cream shirt and a brown pair of Ashley Bennett shoes. He still felt a little bit hungover when Sheba pulled up outside. "Hi John, you look smart" "Thank you and you look stunning also" she had a blue dress with large cream coloured dots and a crème pair of shoes. "So, what happened?" "I went for a walk and ended up at the Barrel at Ropesmoor". "Oh no, is Cole still running the pub?" "Yes, do you know him?" "We went to junior school together and I have been to the pub a few times, great guy but if he gets you drinking it can be a disaster which I'm sure you found out" and she laughed flashing a perfect white set of teeth.

They arrived at the Spinning Jenny and to John' surprise Saron was there but with a smartly dressed guy. "Hey John, are you going to the engagement party?" "Yes, are you?" "Yes, Jimmy asked me and said to bring along a guest, this is Russell Peters". "Pleased to meet you Russell" John said shaking his hand but secretly wanting to crush it. John introduced Sheba to him. "So, tell me, how did you two meet?" "I'm staying at the pub, I'm an electrical engineer and I work for Pippa's Frozen Foods in their Belfast plant but they have some new machinery that I am overseeing, you probably guessed at my accent, I'm from Ireland". He actually seemed a decent guy but that wasn't the point, John

SMILE

was hoping to eventually get back with
Saron.

"Bus is ready" Lindsay shouted, it was a
sixteen-seat bus so they all piled on to
head off to the Wobbly Man, the venue for
the night, Jimmy and Carol were greeting
the guest's as they arrived.

The bar area was very busy and the
function room also, Caz and Jimmy must
have invited over a hundred people John
thought. "What are you drinking Sheba?"
"I'll get these John, we are having a kitty,
are you joining in?" John could see there
was Bob and Cheryl, Shelley and of
course Jack, Phil and his new girl Linda,
Kev and Doreen, Lindsay and Wez and
Saron and the new guy. He wanted to say
no, feeling embarrassed at his feelings for
Saron and also Sheba had the situation

with Phil to contend with but by now Jack had got John a pint so they were locked in. They sat down and, to be fair, John could see there was only himself feeling awkward. Saron was joking with Russell and Linda was talking to Sheba. "Hey mate, are you ok with this?" he whispered in Phil's ear. "Yeah mate, we are still friends so no worries". John thought he'd best just get on with it.

"Come on John, I love this to dance to, "Living Off The Wall" Michael Jackson. Maybe in a bit I can moon dance" and he laughed. "Well I will take the pretty lady if you don't mind John". "Go ahead Russell, fine by me". John watched Russel dancing with Sheba, not only did he seem to be a nice guy with good looks but he could dance as well!!

SMILE

Saron came over to John and chinked her glass on his. "Cheers my dear" she said. "Oh yeah, sorry cheers". "Didn't know you were back seeing Sheba". "I didn't know you had a new boyfriend so I guess we were both in the dark". "Oh Russell? No, I'm not seeing him, he is a nice guy and was at a loose end so I asked if he wanted to come along, guess Sheba was the same hey?" John just smiled at Saron. The night drew on and it was clear Saron was trying to make John jealous, she had really started playing up to Russell as the drinks took effect.

Wez said the bus had arrived so slowly Lindsay rounded them up, Cheryl was a bit wobbly on her feet as Bob helped her on the bus. Saron was draped over Russell and she smiled as she went past John.

Doreen was singing something to Kev it was a bit random but at least she was enjoying it, Jack and Shelly were wedged as they came across the car park and Sheba cuddled up to John on the seat at the front. Kev came around with a collection for the bus driver. The driver then said if anybody wanted to be dropped at their house instead of the pub he would willingly drop them there. Everyone went for that except, of course, Wez and Lindsay.

Saron waved goodbye to John and Sheba as they dropped them in the Tow'd Man car park. Eventually they pulled up at Sheba's house. "Are you staying John?" "Yes, if that's ok". "Of course it is silly or I wouldn't have asked. We can get a taxi for my car in the morning John if you

SMILE

want?" "I will pick you up Sheba". "Brill Kev thanks, shall we say 10.00 am?".

"Sounds good to me, goodnight you two" Kev said with Doreen singing "you are the sunshine of my life "in Kev's ear.

Once inside Sheba's cottage she was insatiable pulling and tugging at John's clothes, before they knew it they were writhing about on the sheepskin rug in front of the log stove. She kissed every inch of John's body and he did the same. Their pulsating love making went on for over an hour but they could not resist anymore. John lay back feeling quite exhausted. "Where did that come from Sheba?" "Oh, I can be hot when I want" she said letting out a little giggle which made her seem even prettier.

Chapter 5

The following day Kev arrived at spot on 10.00 am to pick John and Sheba up, they got in Kev's new Jaguar XK. "Bloody hell mate, what's this?" "It was my Christmas present to myself for all those hard years in the pub". "Well it's very nice mate". "Are we going to have a couple in the Spinning Jenny John?" "Yes, why not" but just as he said that his phone rang, it was Magic. "Sir I have another set of parents here saying their daughter has gone missing I thought you should know". "You are right Magic, I am on my way make them a coffee".

"Sorry Kev that was work, I have to go in". "No problem mate, I dare say Jack and Bob will be having a swift one". "Thanks for the lift mate". He kissed

SMILE

Sheba, Kev was dropping her at the Spinning Jenny for her car. "Anytime lad you know that".

John got in his motor and set off for Bixton, when he arrived Magic said the parents were in interview room two and he had given them a drink. "Ok, thanks Magic". "Good morning, well, almost afternoon, I'm Detective Inspector John Gammon and I believe you are reporting a missing person?" "Yes, it's our daughter Mr Gammon" said the small bespectacled man. "Ok well let's take some details. You are?"

"Brian Murray and this is my wife Tamisha". Tamisha Murray was a striking woman, she looked Asian and probably a good fifteen years younger than Brian Murray. "What is your daughter's name?"

"Chloe Fammargia". "And it's Chloe that is missing?" "Yes". "How old is Chloe?" "She is seventeen Mr Gammon". "Nice name by the way and very unusual". "Yes, my wife was born in Lokmeassim it's an Island in the Indian Ocean, we met when I was helping construct a school out there we have been married eighteen years now and moved back to the UK when Tamisha was pregnant with Chloe". "Do you have a picture of Chloe we could use?" Tamisha pulled out a beautiful picture of Chloe. "Can I ask, this looks like a professional picture". "Yes, it is, Chloe was asked to do some modelling and they did a portfolio of her but she can't work until she is eighteen, they have strict rules". "What was the name of the Agency?" "In the Buff" run by a lovely woman, Sandra

SMILE

Cullen, Chloe went to them because she has always wanted to be a model".

"Well of course Mr and Mrs Murray we will do everything to find your daughter, have you got a list of friends we could talk to? Had you had a row or anything before she left?" "Well Mr Gammon I must admit I didn't like her boyfriend much". Brian Murray looked uneasy when he said it and it was as if his wife was telling him to shut up. Gammon sensed it and went for Tamisha Murray. "What about you Mrs Murray, did you feel the same?" "Not really Mr Gammon, she is young and wants to enjoy her life, I'm afraid Brian is old school. Her boyfriend has quite a lot of tattoos and a nose stud but lots of kids do today, Brian can't really handle it can you Brian?" "Earing's and stuff are for girls and tattoo's well, I just feel they are not educated printing stuff on their body". "I'm afraid two nights before she disappeared she had been and had three little stars tattooed on her right foot, Brian went ballistic, the boyfriend just said, "Calm down Man no big deal" So he chucked the guy out of the house and sent Chloe to bed". Brian was staring at his wife with contempt. "It's no good giving Mr Gammon half a story Brian". "Your wife is correct. Can I have the name of the boyfriend?" "They call him Krassy, I don't know his surname, he lives on Mumps Hill in a flat, the place used to be a doctors' surgery before they turned it into flats, it's in Micklock Mr Gammon". "Ok, and her friend's?" "Just one really close one, Bethany Henshow, she lives at

SMILE

Churchtown Restaurant in Dilley Dale with her parents".

"Ok Mr and Mrs Murray, thanks for your honesty, let me see what we can do, I will be in touch but should you think of anything that may help us find your daughter call me anytime day or night, here's my card"

 The Murray's left the station. "Wow sir, that was a long chat". "Yes, tomorrow get me the team in the incident room at 9.00am in the morning Magic". "Right, I'm off for a well-deserved pint of Pedigree". "Lucky for some sir!" Magic replied. John got to the Spinning Jenny to find Kev, Phil and Jack just a little bit tipsy. Lindsay was doing the bar so he ordered a round "You'd best do me a double brandy as well, I think I am playing catch up". "Hey John, just the man, we are shutting in half an hour but going into the living quarters to play three card brag are you joining us?". "Certainly am my friend".

Lindsay locked up after half an hour and they retired to Wez's living room. "Ok, Barnsley rules, an open man can't see a blind man, maximum blind bet five pounds. A prile of threes are unbeatable then a prile next of aces right down to two's then Ace King and Queen all same suit etc, rest of it, all same rules. Anybody want a cash loan?" "I'll have two hundred Wez". "Ok Jack, anymore?" "You might as well give us all two hundred". "Ok lads". "Just make sure we have enough float to open tonight Wez!" "Don't panic Lindsay".

SMILE

"Oh yeah, I also forgot to say we only shuffle the pack when a prile comes out. Shall I start?" Wez started dealing, once they all had three Kev immediately looked at his cards. "Chicken" said Jack. "No just a cautious man" "We bloody know that Kev!" "Give over Phil, you had more free drinks off me than I can remember". "I know, that's because it didn't happen" and Phil laughed.

Next to look was Jack and he threw his cards in but Kev carried on until eventually it left John and Kev. John made Kev sweat as he was now five pounds blind and Kev was ten pounds open. "Go on then mate, let's have a look at you". Kev had an eight nine ten. John turned over his first card it was a Queen, the second card was a Jack. "Come on John" shouted Phil. The third card was a ten, "Sorry mate, Ten Joe Green as they say". Kev was crestfallen as John piled up the notes in all about one hundred and ten pounds.

"You are bloody jammy John, gambling, women is there anything you don't shine at?" "Keeping Saron hey mate?" "Bollox Phil". "Keep it nice girls" said Wez.

The rest of the day went pretty much the same way with Kev left with one pound fifty, Phil with almost one hundred and fifty, Wez was up by sixty pounds, Jack down by a hundred and John sat with a stack of money at the table. "Well thanks lads, I enjoyed that". "Glad you did, Doreen will kill me". "You can afford it mate". "Right, who is for champagne?" By now the bar was re-opened, John

SMILE

walked in to see a tall blonde- haired girl
dressed to kill behind the bar. "Oh hi, you
are that detective John Gammon aren't
you?" Before John could say yes Kev
blurted in "yeah and a jammy git too".
"I'm Laura Slooter the new barmaid" and
she held out her hand for John to shake
but, being a gentleman and now full of
beer and happiness from the card game, he
kissed her hand, Laura blushed. "Watch
him love or you might get more than you
bargained for". "Be quiet Phil" "Just
warning her mate, that's all".
Laura was quite tall with long legs which
she showed off to her best advantage by
wearing a micro mini skirt. "Stop
slobbering Kev". "I know, way too young
for me Jack". "He wouldn't have a bloody

chance anyway with Gammon about and Doreen in the wings hey mate?"

John just had a silly grin on his face as the alcohol was taking effect. Slowly but surely the lads went home leaving Laura behind the bar and Lindsay cleaning around, even Wez had bailed out.

"So Laura where are you from?" "Well, my parents were living in Spain and I moved out there when my husband and I split up three years back". "Oh, sorry to hear that". "Not a problem, he was an arse anyway Mr Gammon". "John, please, call me John". "Ok John". "So what made you come back?" "I got a job working for the government". "Where is that then?" "Manchester, I commute every day, I live in Swinster, I found I wasn't getting to know anybody and I heard Lindsay was

SMILE

looking for bar staff so I thought ideal to be paid and I will meet people".
"You are quite famous aren't you?" "No, probably infamous is nearer the mark Laura". "So, have you got a boyfriend?". "No, not really had time, I only moved into the village six month ago when I got this job".
John didn't know why but he came straight out and asked if she fancied going out one night. "Oh, ok, I am off on Wednesday, I need to get a doctor and a dentist sorted so if you fancy showing me the highlife of the Peak District that would be fun". "Ok, shall we say Wednesday night 7.30pm?" "Thanks, I will look forward to it".
John called it a night and went home. The following morning there had been a

tremendous storm during the night everywhere was drenched. As John drove to work he could see some tin roof barns were no longer in one piece, John had slept through it so it was a bit of a surprise seeing the devastation.

He arrived at the station and asked Magic if he had sorted the meeting with the team. "Yes Sir, they all know 9.00am in the incident room". Gammon grabbed a coffee and headed for the room armed with pictures of the missing girls which he pinned up on an incident board. Slowly they trickled in and eventually they had all arrived.

"Ok thanks everybody, as you can see our current case is a bit of an odd one and may amount to nothing but let's see where it takes us shall we.

SMILE

The first girl reported missing was Chelsea Much, it has been over a week now since her parents reported her missing. In this time, they did receive a very small video of her distressed in a room before it was cut off, we estimated this to be the derelict flour mill known locally as Bagshaw's Mill at Rowksly. Wally, anything found there?" "Plenty of finger prints but it's used as a bit of a love nest for young one's plus it was a flour mill so there are prints everywhere from its former workforce". "So, nothing you can give us?" "No nothing unless this escalates then I suppose we could go through all the prints but that would take weeks". "Ok, thanks Wally.

Second disappearance reported was that of Keri Vaney" and Gammon pointed to her picture. "Apparently a bit of a wildcat, her parents were killed when she was young, her grandmother brought her up and found her very difficult.

Third disappearance is Chloe Fammargia Murray of mixed parents, Brian and Tamisha Murray, they admitted that Brian Murray had a big fall out over a tattoo his daughter had on her right foot depicting three shooting stars, he also fell out with her boyfriend known only as Krassy.

So, what do we have? three runaways', three alien abductions or three over reacting parents. Or maybe just maybe somebody abducting these girls for money or pleasure which is it?"

"Ok DI Milton, I want you and DI Lee to do some door to door stuff, ask questions, all the usual, let's get some profile about

SMILE

these girls. I don't want to shake the tree too much at this point and start scaring people thinking we have some nut case on the loose when it could just be a case of wilful teenagers".

"DS Bass you come with me, we are going to see the friend of the third girl, she lives in Dilley Dale. The rest of you, normal police work, we don't want to spend too much resource on this as yet for obvious reasons. Ok that's the update thanks".

"Come on Kate, let's go and talk to Bethany Henshow". "Where does she live sir?" "Just on the outskirts of Dilley Dale, her parents own Churchtown Manor".

"Oh, that is that really expensive restaurant isn't it?" "That's the one Kate, I've only been once but the chef Andre Henshow cooks some fabulous stuff and his wife Christina is excellent at front of house".

They drove down the sweeping entrance to the old manor house and proceeded to reception. "Good morning" said the young girl on reception "how may I help you?" "Well actually we are looking for Bethany Henshow, is she around?" and John flashed his warrant card. "Just a moment, I will check". A few minutes passed and Mrs Henshow came to the front desk. "Are you wanting to talk to our Bethany?" "If we could please Mrs Henshow". "Well if you see her I would like to as well!!" "I'm sorry?" "Well, she told us she had a modelling job in Portugal for a couple of weeks, that was five week ago". "Are you getting any communication from Bethany?". "Not a sausage, you know

SMILE

kids, they live on their phones that is until you ring them then it's, oh I missed your call, Mr Gammon".

"Is there somewhere we could talk?" "Yes of course, come into my office". They entered a neat little office with the usual stuff on the walls, holiday planner, shift rota's etc. "You are worrying me Mr Gammon, is there a problem?" "We are unsure at the minute but you are the third person whose daughter has stopped communicating". "Really?" "Yes, we found about Bethany because of Chloe Murray, her parents reported her missing". "To be honest both me and Andre don't like Bethany hanging about with Chloe and that boyfriend, Krassy they call him, I think they are a bad influence Mr Gammon." "Could we have a picture of

Bethany?" "Certainly" and Christina took the picture of Bethany from her desk and gave it to DS Bass. "For about a year now she has lost interest in school and it's ever since Chloe got into this modelling thing". "Did she go to the agency In the Buff?" "Yes she did Mr Gammon, I'm not saying anything is wrong with the agency, they were very professional and Sandra Cullen was spot on, they did a portfolio of her but said they would not put her on their books until she was eighteen. I remember her saying it was good that we came a long because the girls tend to give false names and addresses". "Look we don't want you to worry Mrs Henshow, just keeps us informed if Bethany contacts you please, this is my number, I can be contacted anytime day or night". "Ok Mr Gammon,

SMILE

oh, just to let you know, we are having a French evening if you and your pretty wife would like to book, I'm only saying because places will soon go". "Ok thanks for that Mrs Henshow".

"What a nice lady and such a lovely place to dine". "Yes, I went a couple of months back for the first time, I can highly recommend it Kate". "I'm sorry if I am being nosey sir but I thought you were single?" "I am, Mrs Henshow just assumed I guess".

"Ok, let's get back, we've not learned a lot from that visit I'm afraid". John started the engine and his phone rang. "Oh that's all we need Tom, are you there? we are on our way, me and DS Bass will see you there, make sure Wally and his team are on the way". "A game-keeper stumbled

across a body on Stinton Estate grounds
Kate, that was DI Stampfer with the news,
we'd best go straight there".
Stinton Estates owned huge amounts of
land around Swinster and the surrounding
areas, it was mainly for shooting for the
posh fraternity.
Stampfer had said the body was found at
Fawn Hollow. Fawn Hollow was an
idyllic area, the trees gave great cover for
the deer and there was a small picnic site
and parking as you pulled in.
The weather had turned quite nasty and
the clouds showed dark aggression like
they could erupt into a torrential downpour
at any minute.
"Oh Sir, what a beautiful area". "Yes, we
would sometimes come here me and my
brother with my parents to watch the deer

SMILE

and you could get a tea and cake at that little kiosk but it looks like that's shut now".

"I can see Wally's tent, let's leave the car here, it looks like DI Stampfer is already talking with the Gamekeeper. You go and get some details while I speak with Forensics". "Ok Sir".

"John how many times have I told you about sticking that big fat head in my forensic tent?". "Sorry mate, what have we got?" Wally came out, "female, unsure of age yet, she has been severely beaten and whoever did this cut her mouth on both sides, I am afraid the poor girl looks like the Joker out of the Batman films. I can't tell you much else but yes, I will have a report for 9.00am in the morning I guess". "No Wally, just bring the report to my office please, I'm afraid this could get out of hand and the last thing we need is a press frenzy if this gets out". "Ok mate, whatever you want".

"That's the John Gammon we love, Mr Maverick" and Wally laughed ducking his head back under the tent. Gammon went back to the game-keeper, he showed his warrant card. "What bloody nutcase would do that to a young girl? I don't know what the world is coming too". "I have to agree Mr?" "Eric Stanton". "Have you asked Mr Stanton all the details we need DI Stampfer?" "Yes and DS Bass has them written down". "Ok then we can let Mr Stanton get on with his day, we may need to speak to you again Mr Stanton". "Call me Eric, everybody else does". "Ok Eric,

SMILE

thanks for your help and sorry for your unfortunate find".

Gammon left DS Bass doing house to house with DI Stampfer and headed back to Bixton to get DCI Burns up to speed. It was now almost 4.00pm and the weather had turned really nasty, it was lashing down as John entered Bixton Police Station.

DCI Burns was wading through a mountain of paperwork when Gammon explained about the young girl with her face cut like the Joker from Batman. "John what is wrong with these people?" "I don't know Heather but what I do know is we do our job and the courts give them soft sentences because of over-crowding". "Anyway John, the Court Case is on Tuesday, the prosecutor said we will only be in court for the first day but I have provisionally booked two days at the hotel just in case". "Ok, are we going on the train from Derby?" "Yes, I will meet you there".

SMILE

Chapter 6

Tonight was the night John was seeing the new barmaid at the Spinning Jenny, Laura Slooter, he sort of regretted asking her out as she was quite a bit younger and if Saron or even Sheba got a whiff he would be in trouble, no way out now so he called her and said he would pick her up on the Spinning Jenny car-park about 5.30pm.

Laura was waiting, she had a denim mini skirt with a blouse and denim cropped jacket and a pair of trainers not John's usual type of woman he thought. "Where are you taking me?" she said in a bubbly outgoing way. "Just a tour of the Peak District pubs Laura if that's ok?"
A pub John hadn't been to in many years was the Little Midget, a really tiny pub on

the way to Cramford Moor, they set off
but had only got three miles away when
his phone rang, it was DI Milton. "John
there has been another murder, this time at
Hangman's gate in Puddle Dale, I have
sent Wally and forensics and I am on my
way". "Ok Carl thanks, I will be there in
30 minutes". "Laura, I am really sorry but
that was work and I have to take you
back". "No problem John, maybe another
time" she said as he dropped her at the
Spinning Jenny car park.

Gammon headed to Puddle Dale feeling a
bit relieved at the call from Carl, she was a
bit too young for John and not really his
type but a lovely girl all the same.

Gammon could see Wally's tent blowing
in the wind as he arrived at Hangman's
gate in Puddle Dale so called because the

SMILE

road was the main road to Manchester and they hung Highway Men there as a warning to others.

Gammon had a quick word with DI Milton and said he would be back in a minute to speak to the guy that found her. Wally was just coming out of the tent. "Bloody hell John, they are queuing up, same disfigurement, her face has been cut either side of her mouth. Do you still want all the details kept quiet?" "No mate, make it 9.30am tomorrow in the incident room, that's two now". Gammon rang the station and told PC Magic to organise all officers to a meeting in the incident room at 9.30 am in the morning.

Gammon wandered over to speak to the witness, he flashed his warrant card.

"Good evening sir, I believe you called the

station after you found this poor girl?".
"Yes, I did". "What's your name sir".
"Glyn Doolan" "Do you live in the area?"
"Yes". "Would you mind telling me where
please?" Gammon didn't like the guy's
attitude, he was a rough looking guy, he
had a checked lumberjack shirt over what
looked like had once been a white tee shirt
but was now quite dingy, he had old
corduroy trousers and a pair of wellingtons
that had seen better days.
"I live in Shimwell, sheltered
accommodation". "So, you are of
pensionable age then Mr Doolan?". "No
that isn't the case anymore, anyway, why
do you need all this? I called Bixton
station, I have told that man everything I
know" and he pointed at DI Milton.

SMILE

"Well we just need to get the facts right. When you found the girl, what was the time?" "Oh, I don't know, quarter past six I'm guessing". "Hangman's gate is now quite a remote place since they diverted the road so why would you be there?". Doolan hesitated for a second. "Is there a problem Mr Doolan?"

"Well, don't arrest me, I was checking my rabbit traps". "Your rabbit traps?" "Yes" and he produced a dead rabbit freshly skinned from under his dirty lumber jacket. "So, did you skin that yourself?" "Yes, it takes about thirty seconds". "So, you would have a knife on you is that correct?" "Well I can't skin a rabbit with a stick now can I?" "Can you show me the knife please?" Doolan produce quite a big knife with a blade on one side and a jagged blade at the other side. "DI Milton I want this knife for evidence". Milton produced a clear evidence bag. "If you take my knife I'm stuck". "Sorry Mr Doolan, when we have done tests you will be handed it back dependent on results. Just one last question, was the victim alive when you found her?" Again, he hesitated to answer. "No, I don't think so". "Ok Mr Doolan, we will be in touch". "When do I get my knife back?" "In due course sir". Doolan muttered something derogatory as he walked away. "Do you think he might be involved?" I'm not sure Carl but he is certainly handy with a knife, the bit I'm not getting is the remoteness of the places we are finding these girls, what the hell are they doing in these places? Anyway Carl, call it a night, we can't do much here

SMILE

and Wally is almost finished". "Ok see you in the morning meeting".

John drove straight back home, DC was waiting, anyone would think you haven't got any food fuss cat, he picked her up and began stroking her. It was nice the cat seemed to make the place a home not just somewhere to sleep.

He made a sandwich of ham, lettuce and tomato and a strong cup of coffee and headed to bed, it had been a long day.

The following morning the weather was really dreadful again so John stuck to the main road which took him past Beryl's Butties and that was one place he couldn't resist so he called in. There were about fifteen people in, a mix of builders and truck drivers so he stood out like a sore thumb in his suit. He ordered the doorstep bacon butty and a strong coffee, he was just about to take a bite when a small balding guy, unshaven, came across. "John Gammon isn't it?" "Yes, that's correct" John said with no idea who the guy was. "Don't you remember me?" John looked again, the guy had both front teeth missing and was in what looked to be builder clothes.

"I'm sorry, I'm not very good with placing faces with names". "Brian, Brian Bone". John was still struggling. "I was big mates with your Adam until the family moved to Liverpool for my dad's job". "Blimey of course, Brian Bone, been a lot of years Brian". "Aye and it looks like they have been kinder to you" and he laughed showing the big gap in his teeth.

SMILE

"How is Adam? keep meaning to go and see him, your Mum and Dad still have the farm? What do you do estate agent looking at the suit?" "No, I'm a DI at Bixton Police". "Oh, best watch me tongue then! Bet your Adam is still farming isn't he? he loved the farm". "No, I'm afraid Adam is no longer with us or Mum and Dad". "Oh I am sorry John, what happened?" "Well it's a long story, what are you doing back here?" "I work for Hayles Construction in Ackbourne, just labouring John".

It wasn't until John left that Hayles Construction came into his head, that was where Graham Much worked as a brickie, was this a co-incidence? Gammon arrived at the station and went straight into the incident room for the meeting, Brain Bone had made him almost late for the meeting. "Ok everybody sorry for the delay, we have now two bodies, Wally, would you like to tell us what you have" "Ok, the first victim was Lizzie Tuffs, she was murdered and her mouth cut either side as if she had a smile like the Joker in the Batman films, there was no sign of any sexual interference with the body. The second young girl was Bethany Henshow, again mutilated at the mouth with a sharp knife but no sexual contact evident. DI Gammon gave me a knife also to check from one of the witness's, there is no DNA from the victim on the knife but there was blood from what I believe was a rabbit" "What was approximate time of death of both girls Wally?" "The first

SMILE

victim I would say about four days ago, the latest victim had been dead approximately four hours when we were inspecting her".

"Ok everyone", Gammon put the mutilated pictures up, "I want Glyn Doolan bringing in, DI Milton bring him in for questioning, I'm not sure he is telling us everything. You go with DI Milton DS Yap, DI Lee you come with me, we'd best let the parents know about their children before the frenzy starts". Gammon and Lee headed for Lizzie Tuffs house in Rowksly, they knocked on the door and her boyfriend Craig answered. "Oh, hello Mr Gammon, I'm afraid Lizzie is on a modelling job". "May we come in?" Craig showed them into the living room, Gammon's eyes were immediately drawn to a credit card bill on the coffee table, it was addressed to a Craig Belmont and the amount owed was eighteen thousand, Belmont scooped it up and Gammon could see he hadn't wanted him to see it.

"So how can I help you gentlemen?" "I'm afraid we are calling with a bit of bad news, please sit-down Craig. I'm afraid Lizzie Tuffs has been found dead".

"What? how can she be she is in Turkey". "I'm afraid not sir" said DI Lee. "She was found murdered at Fawn Hollow I'm afraid". "I don't know where that is Mr Gammon". Gammon thought it strange how he emphasised he didn't know where Fawn Hollow was, there was more to this guy than was being portrayed. "Are you

SMILE

ok to answer a few questions?" "Yes, I am
ok"

"So, Craig Belmont, where are you from?"
"I was born in Suffolk but had ten years of
my life at a public school in Lincolnshire
then I went to Durham University to study
photography and eventually got a job for a
company called Curvy Models in
Manchester, I met Lizzie and she was fed
up of travelling to Manchester at a
weekend so I packed my job in and came
to live here with Lizzie". "Where do you
work now?" "I stack shelves at
Morrison's" "Bit of a come down Mr
Belmont?" "Not really, I do nights so have
plenty of time to do my photography".
"Ok, you will need to formally identify
Miss Tuffs, can you make it in
tomorrow?" "Yes, not a problem Mr

Gammon". "Thank you for your time Mr Belmont, we will be in touch".

They left Rowksly and on the way Gammon called DS Bass. "Kate, I want everything finding out about a Craig Belmont, Lizzie Tuffs boyfriend. He was originally born in Suffolk but spent his formative years at a public school in Lincolnshire before moving to Manchester, first as a photographer for Curvy Models, he now lives in Rowksly and works stacking shelves in Morrison's". "Ok Sir leave it with me". "You are not impressed with Craig Belmont are you John?" "Something doesn't quite shape up, did you clock the credit card bill.?" "Actually, I didn't". "It was for over £18,000 Peter". "Wow." "Anyway, I might be wrong but something

SMILE

isn't clicking with me on this guy. Can't say I am looking forward to going to see the Henshows Peter, they are a nice couple, such a massive shame". "Yes, I have heard good reports about their restaurant". "Yes, it is very good, this will devastate them".

Gammon and Lee drove up the drive of Churchtown Manor, Gammon parked in the car park and they walked around, Christina was on the front desk. "Hey Mr Gammon lovely to see you again". "Is your husband here at the minute Christina?" "Yes, why?" "Could you get him please, is there somewhere private we can talk?"

"Come here into the back office and I will fetch Andre Mr Gammon". The small office at the back of the red caption desk

had two chairs and a desk with a couple of
family pictures of when Bethany was
about twelve on a skiing trip with her
Mum and Dad.

Andre and Christina arrived.

"Please you two, take a seat". "What's this
about, what as my Andre done?" "Nothing
Mrs Henshow, this is about your daughter
Bethany. I am afraid Bethany has been
found murdered at Puddle Dale". "No"
Christina cried, "No, you must be
mistaken" Andre comforted her. The poor
woman was absolutely in bits. "Peter fetch
Mr and Mrs Henshow a glass of water
each please".

"I'm afraid I am going to have to ask you
to formally identify Bethany at the morgue
tomorrow, I am sorry to say she has been
facial disfigured" "Was she attacked?" "If

SMILE

you mean sexually then no, we found no evidence of any sexual contact".

DI Lee came back with two glasses of water but poor Christina was shaking so bad she couldn't hold the glass, Andre had to do it for her. "Would you like a grief councillor to come over? I can arrange that Andre". "No Mr Gammon, we have each other but thank you". "Ok then, we will leave you to grieve Andre". Gammon looked at poor Christina with her whole world turned upside down by some flippin nutcase.

"Ok Peter, let's get back, hopefully DS Bass has something positive for us after that". "It never gets any easier John does it?". "It certainly doesn't mate". They arrived back at Bixton and John went straight to see DS Bass. "Any joy Kate?"

"Still working on it Sir, can I have
everything ready for morning?" "Ok, I just
don't want the trail to go cold". "Promise I
will stay and have all the details for you".
"Ok Kate, thanks". John did some of his
paperwork then called it a night there were
only a few more days before Seward's
trial.

He headed for the Spinning Jenny to see if
Lindsay would do him a take out, Tracey
Rodgers was behind the bar. "Evening Mr
Gammon". "Evening Miss Rodgers, a pint
of Pedigree please". "Coming up". "You
on your own tonight?" "Should have been
that new girl Laura but apparently she has
had an upset tummy all day so she told
Wez she wasn't going to be able to work
so they called me and asked me to fill in".

SMILE

"Well you are a great replacement". "Give over Gammon with the smoothie talk" and she laughed tossing her long hair backwards. "Are you going on that short break to Rome?" "Not heard about it Trace". "Two weeks' time, Lindsay got it up, shall I put your name down?" "Who's going?" "Well at the minute there is Jack and Shelley, Lindsay and Wez, Me and India". "Is Steve going?" "No, he said he wasn't bothered so India asked me". "Oh well that should be nice, anyone else?" "Apparently Saron is going with some guy called Russell who is staying at the Tow'd Man and working at Pippa's Frozen Foods as a contractor, then I think Bob and Cheryl are going and Tony and Rita". "Stick my name down" "Just one?". "Yep, the original Billy No Mates me Tracey".

"Yeah, likely Gammon" and she laughed as she added John to the list.

The pub was reasonably busy and Lindsay did his take away, Barnsley chop, mashed potatoes, roast potatoes, green beans, carrots and cauliflower cheese.

John paid Tracey for the food, thanked Lindsay and set off home. Little DC came rushing to the cat flap waiting for John to open the door then she was wrapped around his legs, purring for all it was worth.

"Come on then DC" the cat followed him while he poured a large Jameson's and put his dinner in the microwave for ten minutes, when he sat at the table the cat jumped up and curled up on his knee, contented that John was back.

SMILE

The following day DS Bass was waiting for John. "All done Sir". "Well done Kate, let me get a coffee and we can go through it". Bass looked up to Gammon, he was the detective she dreamed of being one day, he was always so cool she thought. "Ok Kate, what have you got for me?" "Well sir, Craig Belmont was born into quite a rich family, he was sent to boarding school then did photography. Belmont has done some big photo shoots, he worked with GQ, Hollow and Ok magazines, apparently work dried up when he was a director at Curvy Models. He was known in the industry as a very good photographer but he had a penchant for younger girls, one girl, wait for it sir, was Keri Vaney, apparently she complained to GQ magazine that Belmont had been

suggestive at a shoot in Jamaica, because
of that Curvy Models lost the contract and
very quickly the others dropped the
agency, Belmont was dismissed as a
director sir".
"I checked his bank account and he is
living on a five- thousand-pound
overdraft, he has three credit cards, two
are maxed out on ten thousand each and
one he owes eighteen thousand three
hundred on". "That's the one I saw Kate,
he is living way beyond his means for
somebody stacking shelves at Morrison's,
let him stew a couple of days, let's go and
see the owner of Curvy Models".
Gammon and Bass headed for Manchester,
well, the outskirts actually, Ancoats and
the address 16 Stodge Lane. "Bloody hell,
it's shut down, look sir, here on the

SMILE

window it say's "WE HAVE
RELOCATED TO ACKBOURNE HIGH
STREET UNDER NEW
MANAGEMENT AS IN THE BUFF" Its
signed by Raznak Bolan"
"Maybe this hasn't been a total waste of
time after all". They drove back to Bixton
and it was almost 5.30pm, Gammon told
Bass to meet him in the car park at In The
Buff model agency at 9.00am the
following day.
The following day was the day Gammon
and Burns were travelling to London so he
rang Heather and said he would meet her
there as this had come up.
Gammon stopped at Costa Coffee situated
across from In the Buff Model Agency, he
ordered a coffee and sat in the window
waiting on DS Bass. Bass arrived spot on

9.00am and Gammon hurried outside, they walked across the road to the agency. Sandra Cullen was already at the reception desk. "Good morning, I wondered if we could have a word". "Look Mr Gammon this is getting a bit like harassment and I really don't have time for detective games". "I understand, would you rather do this at the station?"

"What do you want?" "I want to know about Raznak Bolan". "What exactly do you want to know?" "He is registered as a director of this company?". "Yes, along with me, Clive Winch and Alan Rose and company secretary Aileen Stope".

"So, tell me what they all do" "Raznak mainly works from Bulgaria finding models throughout Europe, Clive Winch and Alan Rose do all the photography and

SMILE

I do all the administration etc". "What about the Company Secretary?". "Aileen looks after the finance side but works mainly from home in Suffolk, she comes up for board meetings as does Raznak". "So, when is your next board meeting Sandra?" Gammon was getting the impression that Sandra Cullen was straight there was no sign of lying or under handedness.

"Look Sandra I will get straight to the point, we have two young girls that have been murdered, both girls have ties to this agency, one of the girl's boyfriend worked at Curvy Models in Manchester which is now closed but gives this agency as its premises". "Which it would Mr Gammon, we bought the model book off them when they shut so their girls are on our books".

"Were you a Director of Curvy Models?"
"No, I believe Craig Belmont was but he
has nothing to do with us, he was
dismissed from Curvy Models". "So, what
about Raznak Bolan?". "He approached us
and said the company was failing big time
since the incident with Belmont and young
Varney and that most of the customers had
dropped him, we already knew that
because they had come to us. We offered
Raznak a position as, to be fair, it wasn't
his fault and he has good contacts in
Europe".
"So, would you say Raznak Bolan is an
honest guy?". "Well I certainly hope so!".
"I didn't ask you that Sandra" "Well if I
am honest, I had my reservations because
of the trouble, I didn't want our reputation
being tarnished but Alan and Clive said it

SMILE

was too good an opportunity to miss so I was voted down as they say. Raznak's name doesn't appear on any of our correspondence, just in case Mr Gammon". "Ok Sandra well thank you for your time".

Gammon told Bass he was heading to London and to put a tail on Belmont during the day, hopefully he would be back by the end of the week.

Gammon left his car at Derby Station and got the train to St Pancras then a taxi across London to the hotel where he was meeting Heather for dinner. The Cosgrove Hotel was a plush five-star hotel close to the Courts of Justice. Gammon showered and changed then headed down to see Heather in reception at 8.30pm.

John had never seen Heather really dressed up but she was tonight. "Looking very sparkly tonight Heather" "Why thank you Mr Gammon". The waiter showed them to their table in the ornate dining room.

"John, I am quite nervous about tomorrow". "It's nothing Heather, just stand up and tell the truth and you will be fine". "Fingers crossed John". The food arrived and it was magnificent. "Hope I can get this through expenses John". "They never question when you are a witness at a big trial, stop worrying". They called it a night and John said he would see Heather at 9.30am for the short walk to the Court. They arrived and were met by an official and taken into a side room. "Is there a problem?". "I am afraid

SMILE

Mr Seward has been found with his throat cut and there will be no trial". "What!! How the hell can that happen was he not under protected custody?" "I can't answer your question DCI Burns but there is no trial I can assure you". "Well that's us done Heather, best get back to Derbyshire" "Does this happen a lot John?" "Well he has upset some very important underworld people Heather, I'm not surprised to be honest".

It was almost 6.00pm when John jumped in his car and headed for the Spinning Jenny. John walked in, there was Carol and Jimmy with Jack and Shelley, Bob and Cheryl and Rita and Tony. "We were just saying John might be in, we fancy a game of Jacks, you up for it?" "Of course he is aren't you my favourite copper?"

Carol said. Jimmy just gave a silly grin.
"Go on then". "There you go old lad, a
pint of Pedigree to take to the table"
"What are you playing?" "Man's game
Wez". "Ha ha, I'll join in then". Just then
Kev and Doreen came in, "Count us in as
well". "Ok Wez, you deal a card to each
person until a Jack comes out, that person
names a drink, brandy, whisky, something
like that, then you deal again and the
second Jack names a drink into the same
glasses, oh and the glass is never washed.
The third Jack out pays for the two drinks
and the fourth Jack has to drink it down in
one, if they don't they have to buy a
round". "Sounds like my kind of game
Cheryl" and he laughed.
First game, John and Chery chose Brandy
and Baileys Jimmy had to pay and Carol

SMILE

had to drink it, this went on until almost midnight when Lindsay came out to see where Wez was. Wez had won a lot of drinks and was now quite incoherent, Cheryl was almost under the table with Bob not much better. John and Jack hadn't won many but paid for quite a few. Shelley had wobble gob and could not get her words out. Lindsay arranged taxis for everyone except John who said he only won two drinks all night.

The following day Gammon arrived to chaos in the Station. "Good morning sir" "What is that commotion?". "Sorry sir, I would have rung you but I didn't know you were back. Mr French came into the station last night a bit shaken, he said he had heard a scream while out walking his dog in Clough Dale and he found a young girl barely alive, she had been cut across her mouth like the other victims. I sent John Walvin and the team with DI Smarty to the scene, a Mrs Tink, owner of the Lodge, had also been out walking the dog and she identified the victim as Chelsea Much, somehow word got to Chelsea's parents and Mr Much said he is going to sue Bixton police and DI Gammon, that's what the commotion is, they are in interview room one with DI Smarty and DI Lee, trying to calm them down". "Did the girl survive?" "Apparently not sir" "Did anybody speak with her?" "Apparently Mrs Tink did but DI Smarty said she was in shock and you might want to speak to her".

"Ok, thanks Magic, I'd best get in there". Gammon entered the room and he got the

SMILE

impression Graham Much was ready to strike him, Dave Smarty calmed him down.

"John Gammon you are a charlatan, you told us not to go to the media with this and now our daughter is dead, how many more families are going to suffer our hurt before you find this maniac?". Gammon was a bit shocked at how Graham Much had gone from basically a boring guy to this irate monster he saw in front of him. "Mr Much I only advised you with your daughter's best interests at heart, we are all deeply saddened at what has happened I can assure you". Well be assured about this Gammon, every newspaper in the country will descend on Bixton and you and this Keystone Cop joke of a police force" and

he brushed past Gammon pulling his
sobbing wife behind him.
As they came out of the Interview room
DCI Burns was at the front desk having
heard the commotion. "My office DI
Gammon" she said in stern manner, the
like of which Gammon hadn't experienced
from Heather Burns.
Gammon followed her up the stairs to her
office. "Shut the door please" she said.
"What the hell was that all about?"
Gammon explained what had happened.
"Bloody hell John, what with yesterday's
mess and now this the last thing I need his
being hung out to dry by the countries
media". "Don't you think I know this
Heather?" "I'm as upset about yesterday
and this situation as you are but we did
everything by the book and if I have to

SMILE

face the wolves tomorrow if Much carries
out his threat then so be it, it won't be the
first time and I doubt very much it will be
the last".

"That's all fine and dandy for you John
but this was a big chance for me in my
career and I don't want it to go down the
pan. There are people in London that want
me to fail, they have said I am not hard
enough on my staff and yes, your name
was mentioned, they questioned if I could
control the maverick John Gammon. I
never told you because we have a good
working relationship and I didn't want that
changing but if I find out the media have
something on this station and our
investigation into Chelsea Much's
disappearance then you will see a different
side of me now please close the door on

the way out". Gammon felt a bit betrayed at Burns outburst as he felt it was unwarranted, he left the office.

"DI Milton bring Craig Belmont in for questioning, tell him he has the option of a lawyer". "Ok on my way". It was almost 11.00am when Belmont's solicitor arrived, Gammon sent in DS Bass to set the machine up and told DI Milton to go in with him.

"Good morning, I'm DI Gammon, this is DI Milton and operating the recorder is DS Bass, you are Havely Wint, Mr Belmont's solicitor?". "Before we go any further DI Gammon I believe you have spoken to my client and he has been one hundred percent cooperative with you, I wish you to also understand Mr Belmont has also had the tragic news that his

SMILE

girlfriend Lizzie Tuffs had been found murdered".

"Ok Mr Wint, that is the reason your client is here today so shall we begin?".

"Can I call you Craig?" "Yes, if you wish". "So, Craig, just so we have a bit of background on you, you are a photographer by trade is that correct?"

"Yes". "What exactly do you photograph?" "The model industry was my forte". "That is interesting but now you stack shelves at Morrison's in Bixton is that correct?" "At the moment yes".

"Do you find that a little demeaning Craig?". "Not in the least, why would I?"

"Well, we have been looking into your past and you were a director at Curvy Models in Manchester is that correct? Is it also correct that you had a complaint made

against you whilst on a shoot in Jamaica?"
"It was a load of rubbish but they believed
her instead of me". "So, this story you
gave me about leaving Curvy Models
because Lizzie Tuffs got fed up of
travelling to Manchester wasn't correct
was it Craig you were dismissed?".
"Look what does that matter?". "Well
Curvy Models lost all the big contracts
didn't they?". "Serves them right". For the
first time Belmont showed some emotion
and his dislike for Curvy Models. "So, the
guy who finished you was Raznak Bolan
is that correct?". "Yes, he told me to
resign". "So, am I safe to say you don't
like Mr Bolan?". "Not bothered either
way". "Well we now find out that Raznak
Bolan is a director at In The Buff Model
agency, the very one who all the murder

SMILE

victims so far have had an association with".

"What are you trying to say, I killed these girls then my own girlfriend?" "Well to be honest Craig it had crossed my mind and killing the girlfriend would seem odd to some people don't you think?" Belmont's solicitor asked if they could take a break of five minutes.

Gammon, Milton and Bass grabbed a coffee. "Did you look at any insurance policies that have been taken out by Craig Belmont?" "No sir". "Ok Kate, get off and do that DI Milton can run the machine, try and be quick Kate". "Will do sir" Gammon and Milton went back and Milton started the tape. "Let's talk about your financial situation". Belmont smiled. "Have I said something funny?" "No, it's just that I know what you are going to say". "Well you have approximately fifty-eight thousand pounds worth of debt over three credit cards, that seems an awful lot to have for a guy stacking shelves in Morrison's, would you agree Craig?" "Yes, it's a lot of money but I am due an inheritance that is going to probate at the minute from my Aunty June, it will be about eighty-five thousand pounds so the debt isn't a worry". "Oh I see, lucky man hey?" Gammon said sarcastically.

"Mr Gammon what more do you want from my client, he has told you everything you have asked so is there anything else?". "For now, no Mr Wint, your client is free to go but we may need to speak to him again as our investigations progress, good day to you". Gammon left the room and

SMILE

headed to Heather Burns to tell her what had been said, he knocked and a tearful Burns asked him to come in and shut the door. "Whatever is a matter Heather?" "John can I apologise for my manner towards you earlier?" "Don't be silly, I am professional enough to know how much hassle you are getting Heather but we will get the perpetrator trust me on that".

"I have just had the Micklock Mercury on, a Billy Hutchinson". "That weasel, what does he want?". "He wants to come and see me, he said if he gets an exclusive it will put the media wolves off tomorrow". "Let him come in Heather". "He was so nasty John". "Look, me and Hutchinson go a long way back, we will handle him". Five minutes later there was a knock on Burns door. "Yes PC Magic?"

"Your visitor is here ma'am, I have put him in interview room two, would you like drinks?" "Coffee for me Magic" "Just a bottle of water please. Did you get Mr Hutchinson a drink?" "Yes ma'am, he had an orange juice". "Ok, we will be down in a minute". "Just let him stew Heather for a couple of minutes. Oh, I am going on a long weekend to Rome next weekend so will need Friday and Monday off if that's ok?". "Of course John, you rarely take any days off, we must owe you loads!!"
"Come on, let's get this over with". They entered the room and Hutchinson got up, he shook Heather Burns hand and offered his hand to Gammon, Gammon didn't accept and sat down. "Not feeling friendly Mr Gammon?". "Detective Inspector Gammon to you Hutchinson now what do

SMILE

you want?". "I am told tomorrow they will be descending on you like a plague of locust from the media so here is my deal, you give me an exclusive insight into the case and the media boys are goosed because you can't talk about it". "That sounds good Mr Hutchinson but what exactly do you want?"

"Well, I will tell the waiting press boys that he Micklock Mercury have exclusivity on the case so it's pointless waiting around, you give me that exclusivity". "What, you think we will share how a murder case is going are you having a laugh Hutchinson?".

"What I want DI Gammon is the name of a suspect and the name of a victim before it is released and a few bits more when you get the person, I think that's a fair swap, its either that or I am with this mob tomorrow calling for DCI Burns and DI Gammon's heads. I can see the headline now, "BURNT GAMMON LET'S THROW IT AWAY" DCI Burns and DI Gammon are inept, it's time we had a police force to be proud of not this bungling double act". "Right that's it Hutchinson, I have heard enough". Gammon got up but DCI Burns took charge. "Look Mr Hutchinson, you scratch our backs we scratch yours, you prove that loyalty in the paper tomorrow with a headline of "BURNS AND GAMMON" working with their team all hours of the day to try and protect our community. We should be proud of Bixton Police working under severe cuts but still maintaining a team dedicated to serve the Peak District

SMILE

with honour and integrity. You write that and add some more and we have a deal Mr Hutchinson". "Not a problem DCI Burns, I will also call off the pack, I will be in touch".

Hutchinson again shook Burns hand but knew better than to offer again to Gammon as he left. "Have you gone mad Heather? that scum ball will do anything for a story". "I know and that's why I told him what to write, he can hardly go back on his own words can he?". "You crafty minx Miss Burns!". "Not just a pretty face DI Gammon" and she laughed as she walked away. Gammon was impressed at Heather Burns turning the situation around on the media, everyday a school day he thought.

Chapter 7

Gammon stood looking out of his window at Losehill thinking about Saron and the guy she was taking to Rome, she hadn't been in touch so he pretty much thought that maybe it was over for them, well I guess I'd best move on he thought, go to Rome, see what fun there is there then take stock when he got back. It was then he remembered that Lisa Tink had spoken to the girl, Gammon grabbed his coat and rushed to Jim and Lisa Tink's house at Clough Dale. He drove up the sweeping drive which had flowers bordering the length of it, Lisa was always tidy and her gardens were really well kept. He knocked on the big oak door of the house, Lisa answered, she looked so pale and her eyes were red raw with crying.

SMILE

"Lisa, how are you?". "Come in John, Jim has gone to a darts meeting, I'm better than I was, I just can't get that pretty girls face out of my mind. Would you like a drink? I'm having a Brandy". "I'll have the same please Lisa, my officer said she was barely alive when you found her, could she speak?". "She could but with great difficulty, she had lost so much blood and her mouth was cut either side so she struggled with her words". "Can you remember what she said?" "I think she said Ireland and incurrence, that's what it sounded like but I can't be sure, then I lost the poor girl. I knew who she was, she had a Saturday job at the hairdresser I used to go too, she was a lovely girl John" and Lisa started to cry again. "Why would anyone what to do this to her? they are so sick". "Well the next question is, did you see anybody?" "No, I think she had been there some time with the amount of blood she had lost".

"Ok Lisa, I know this is no comfort but I will get this person, you can be sure of that". "How are Mr and Mrs Much? I can't begin to think how they must feel". "They are very emotional which is understandable I guess". Lisa poured them both another brandy then John said he would leave her in peace, she said Jim would be back in about an hour.

John headed for the Spinning Jenny to pay for his Rome trip, Lindsay was doing the bar, she said Wez was cooking. "I have come to pay for my Rome trip please Lindsay". "That's brilliant John, we leave Saturday from here at 6.30 am, the bus

SMILE

will take us to East Midlands Airport and we fly direct to Rome, we are stopping at The Grand Melia, it's about a five-minute walk into the centre of Rome so perfect really John". "Sounds great". "Don't think I am being nosey but you do know Saron is going don't you?" "Yes its fine Lindsay, honest". "Ok, I just didn't want you to be surprised that's all". "Thanks for thinking of me", Lindsay smiled and pulled John a pint of Pedigree. It was quiet so John sat and read the Guardian, he had one more beer then left deciding to go and see DC the cat.

DC was at her best, purring and wrapping herself around John's legs, well if nothing else at least Saron got him a cat he thought.

The following day his drive to work
through the back roads was idyllic and
made living in the sticks a joy at times.
John arrived at the station and was met by
a barrage of reporters. "DI Gammon, any
comments on the murder of Chelsea
Much, is it true they are suing the station
for incompetence?" Just then Hutchinson
pulled up. "Guys, over here please, I have
something for you". Gammon watched
from inside the station, within a few
minutes they had dispersed then Billy
Hutchinson did the same. that was quite
impressive Gammon thought.

"Have you seen this sir?" Magic tossed the
Micklock Mercury on the desk, the
headline was "Peak District Murders in the
safest hands" DCI burns and DI Gammon
are well versed in this type of police work.

SMILE

DI Gammon is well known to the readers of this newspaper and when he tells me they will get the perpetrators of these heinous crimes I believe he will he has done it before and the Micklock Mercury has total faith in Bixton police".
"Not a bad write up eh sir?" "Time will tell Magic" he said climbing the stairs to his office and the start of another day.
It was almost time to call it a day when Gammon could hear hysterical screams from down stairs, he rushed out of his office almost knocking Heather Burns down the stairs as she left her office at the same time. There was a young girl with blood dripping from her mouth, Gammon knew straight away it was Keri Varney from the picture he had. "Let me look Keri, what happened?". "I decided to go

back to Grandma's to live so I caught a
bus to Dilley Dale, I only had enough
money to get as far as Dumpling Dale and
knew I had to walk the three miles to
Dilley Dale, I got off the bus". All the
time she was talking, blood was dripping
from a cut to the left-hand side of her face.
"Lucky for me there were quite a few
walkers still about for some reason, I felt
nervous, maybe it was the thought of what
has happened to my friends. I had gone
about a mile when, as I started descending
down the valley, a man grabbed me from
behind, it was Craig Belmont, he slashed
one side of my face and said something
like" You bitch you ruined my life" by
now I was in the bracken and he lunged at
me again, I know he was going to cut me
again. I brought my knee up between his

SMILE

legs and he fell back in pain, I managed to get up and I kicked him twice more between the legs and then I ran, I knew the road was about three hundred yards that I was going to cross, lucky for me a farmer was coming back from market and he stopped and brought me here". "Did he come in with you?" "No, he said he didn't want to get involved and he left me at the door".

"DI Milton you and Yap go and arrest Belmont and get him back here, DS Bass you take Keri to the hospital to get this cut sorted then take her home please". Gammon informed DCI Burns and she said she wanted to be in on the interview, Belmont arrived with his solicitor just before lunchtime.

The first words out of Wint's mouth, Belmont's solicitor were "This better be good DI Gammon, if not I will be taking this way above your heads at this station" "Good for who Mr Wint? It's certainly good for the victims of these horrendous murders as we now have a witness who was attacked at Dumpling Dale and they allege it was your client, Craig Belmont". "That's rubbish" Belmont shouted, jumping to his feet. "Sit down Mr Belmont" said DCI Burns. "Who is this supposed witness?". "Somebody you have history with Craig, Keri Vaney, but she managed to escape you. Do you own a knife?" "What, a steak knife do you mean?" "I was thinking more of a hunting knife perhaps". Belmont whispered to his solicitor. "My client wishes to say that he

SMILE

does own a hunting knife although he has never hunted anything because he doesn't like killing".

"That's rather appropriate Mr Belmont, we have acquired a search warrant for your house and outbuildings, do you own any other properties or rent any other properties, lock ups or garages?" Belmont showed some hesitation before he answered no. "Do you own a car?" "No" he replied. "Are you sure?" "Yes, I'm sure".

"Mr Belmont, I am holding you for forty-eight hours and then I will interview you again". Gammon had the tape stopped, "Mr Wint, if you would like to return in forty-eight hours when a decision will be made on the evidence we have collected, take him to the holding cells please DI

Milton". Belmont was taken away
protesting his innocence, nothing new
there Gammon thought because they all do
that he thought.

"Ok DI Smarty, take DI Stampfer, DI
Finney and DS Bass with Wally's team
and let's have a good look at his house, I'll
be along shortly" Gammon and Burns
went up to Burns office. "Do you think he
is our man John?" "All the evidence so far
is that he is our best bet if Keri Varney
picks him out in a line up I intend to have
after 48 hours, right I'm going to
Belmont's house let's hope we turn
something up".

Gammon arrived at Number four Stinton
Terrace Rowksly, there was a hive of
activity with Wally as usual bemoaning

SMILE

the amount of people around any evidence
he thought he might find.

"DI Smarty, anything so far?". "Well,
there is a car in the garage but it's locked".
"Force the lock, let's get it taken away to
be looked at, check who it's registered to
first though Dave" "Will do".

"Anything yet Wally?" "Loads of finger
prints but I guess there will be plenty of
Lizzie Tuffs, she lived here with him".
"Have you found a hunting knife by any
chance?" "Not yet, am I looking for one
specifically?" "I think it could help us, I
know he had one but he says he has never
used it, if I can prove any of the girl's
faces have been cut with the blade of that
knife we are home and dry".

Gammon decided to leave the scene but
told everyone he wanted results for the

9.00 am meeting tomorrow. Something was getting to Gammon, why had Much suddenly become this nutcase when he had been a boring, mild mannered man before? Was it just emotion or was there a more underlying trend that they hadn't looked into? Gammon headed back to the station with his mind set to look harder into Graham Much.

Gammon sat at his computer going through the police data base but basically, he was looking into the London area. He had been looking for almost three hours when he got a report of a sexual predator called Malcolm Mulch, this man served twelve years in Wandsworth, this man had attacked three women over a period of five years, he hadn't raped anyone but he was very physical with them, black eyes and

SMILE

the like. There was no picture of Michael
Mulch so John rang Danny Dempsey at
Scotland Yard, an old friend.
"Danny?" "John Gammon, how are you".
"I'm ok mate" "Nice to hear from you,
how's life in the sticks?". "Yes, good
mate, how are you?" "I got married two
years back and just had our first son".
"Hey brilliant mate" "We called him
John". "After me I hope" and John
laughed. "Who else mate!!" "Anyway, I
wondered if you can help me, I am
looking to see if a guy called Graham
Much has a record, I have found Malcolm
Mulch who served twelve years in
Wandsworth and just had a hunch it might
be the same guy, maybe moved up here
once his sentence was complete". "Hang
on John, I actually remember that name, a

mate of mine was the arresting officer, give me ten minutes to get the file and I will call you back". "Thanks Danny". Gammon put the phone down and waited, about twenty minutes later Danny called back. "John I have the file, the guy was a bricklayer from Hackney, he had previous convictions for fighting and before he was convicted he had several complaints about touching women levelled at him" "This is all sounding like my man Danny" "There's more John, when he got out he had to report weekly to Hackney police station and he informed them he was moving to Derbyshire with his wife and daughter, Hackney police contacted Derby police and he went in every week for the next four years until he was no longer under those reporting conditions which

SMILE

was about eighteen month ago John. I have copied the picture and have sent it to your phone now". "Brilliant, thanks Danny, I owe you one". "Come and see us soon, would be great to catch up John". "Promise I will, thanks mate".

John opened the picture Danny sent and it was Graham Much although about twenty years older now, John knew it was him, he decided that the following day he was bringing Graham Much in for a chat. It was now almost 5.30pm, Gammon started to pack away and DCI Burns put her head round his door. "Goodnight John, hopefully Wally has turned something up on Belmont for the meeting tomorrow"." If you have a minute Heather". "Sure, what is it?". Gammon explained his hunch about Graham Mulch and what he had found out and that he intended bringing him in tomorrow. "Heather, you look hesitant?" "Just the stink he kicked up with the press, I just wonder if we should monitor him before we question him". "It's your shout Heather". "Well if you don't mind, put DS Yap on him for a week, see if we get anything suspicious". This really wasn't a good idea Gammon thought but Heather is always so supportive he decided to go along with her this time. "Ok John, see you in the morning" "Oh Heather, you haven't forgot I have that short break to Rome this weekend?" "No, I haven't John, have a lovely time, it's a great place to visit". With that Heather left. Gammon finished off and decided to call at the Spinning

SMILE

Jenny to finalise times etc for Friday's trip to Rome.

"Evening Wez". "Hiya John, how's tricks?". "Wish I had some mate". "Hey, you ready for Roma!!" Wez said in an Italian accent, well, that's what he thought he sounded like, it came across somewhere between a Geordie and a Yorkshire accent actually but it made John laugh.

"Hello Pal". "Hey Phil, how are you? been flippin ages". "Yeah had loads of work on but top side now hence a few beers tonight to build up to the Rome trip, so you best have one with me John". "Ok, thanks Phil, a Pedigree please". "How many Euro's do you think we need Wez?" "Well, the hotel is bed and breakfast so you have two more meals to find then any trips you might want to go on and of course the beer money". "So, a lot then!!" Phil said chuckling to himself. "I reckon so mate, forgot to say John, your mate Steve came in the other night with India, he was asking if you were going on the Rome trip as he had told India he wasn't bothered so she is going with Tracey Rodgers, I think he was a bit disappointed, he had planned a few sessions with you John".

"Well it's typical Steve, think's I'm a mind reader, hardly heard a thing from him now he is all loved up with India". "What time do we set off Friday morning?" "Mini bus picks us up at 5.30am from the car park mate, our flight is 10.40am from East Midlands, should be a good weekend". "So, who's going now then?" "Well it's full, me and Linz, Phil

SMILE

and Linda, Jimmy and Carol, Shelley and Jack, Bob and Cheryl, Tony and Rita, India and Tracey, Saron and Paddy". "Paddy?" "Yeah, that guy who is staying at the Tow'd Man and working at Pippa's Frozen Foods, and then there is you, Billy No mates!". "Ha ha, very funny Barnsley Chop"

The night carried on with the usual banter and John said he would see them on Friday morning at 5.30am, with it being Thursday tomorrow he knew he had quite a big day ahead of him so he left the lads drinking in the Spinning Jenny and went home.

Gammon arrived the following day with fingers crossed that Wally had something on Belmont. He was feeling quite positive, in his eyes they had two very good suspects in Belmont and Much, Much though looked like he would have to wait because of DCI Burns order.

The meeting started prompt at 9.00am, Gammon had a lot to do with taking Friday and Monday off so he wanted a result from Wally.

"Ok everybody, we have two very good suspects in my opinion, one we have in custody, Craig Belmont, so first if you could come up Wally and let us know what you have found at his house yesterday please".

Wally came up looking a little hesitant.

"Well I'm afraid we found nothing in my opinion that I would not have expected with him living with one of the victims, we found this knife". Wally showed everyone a large knife with teeth on one

SMILE

side of the blade and a normal side on the other. "The only thing we could find with this is it had a turps residue on the blade and the handle and maybe it had been cleaned. The boys looked at the car, there were Lizzie Tuffs fingerprints everywhere and Craig Belmont's but nobody else's, I'm afraid other than the turps on the blade, nothing to report".

Gammon felt gutted, he was sure they would find something. He got Belmont and his solicitor into the interview room and he asked Belmont about the turpentine used on the knife, he passed that off quite smugly by saying he had opened a tin of paint at some time and it got on the blade and the handle so he cleaned it with turps, Gammon had no choice but to let him go.

He felt totally demoralised and Heather Burns could see that. "John, have your break, you have been working hard on this case, enjoy Rome and come back feeling refreshed, we will get whoever is doing this". "Ok Heather, I know what you are saying, it's just so frustrating". "Look I tell you what, I have a good idea about Graham Much and if I think we are right I will arrange for you to interview him with his solicitor on the Tuesday that you are back at work". "Brilliant Heather". "Right, well, get off and have a great time". "Ok, thanks, see you when I get back". Gammon left work and decided to go straight home sort DC out and pack his bag for his four- day break to Rome. DC was pleased to see him back early and made the usual fuss, John had given a key

SMILE

to Roger Glazeback to just pop in and make sure DC was ok. He had set up an automatic food and water dispenser so that wasn't a problem, he just thought the cat would want a bit of fuss from Roger while he was away.

Chapter 8

The following morning John was up at
4.00am, he showered and shaved, DC
hadn't left his side since he got up, it was
like she knew he was leaving her for a few
days.

John left for the Spinning Jenny pulling
into the car park at the same time as the
mini bus. It was a nice morning, Jimmy
and Carol had a crate of bottles, they
certainly intended having a good time,
they all piled on the bus, John sat with
India, Tracey, Tony and Rita on the back
seats, they were all on except for Saron
and Paddy as they called him but John
didn't want to show any jealousy so he
stuck with correct name of Russell. They
got on the bus, Saron dressed in a tweed
jacket and matching skirt cut just above

SMILE

her knee, she looked a million dollars as usual. They set off for the airport, Lindsay handed out the plane tickets, everyone got their plane passes and set off for security. Saron was talking with Rita and Tony which left Russell and John at the back, the others were through when Russell was held up, apparently his passport was out of date, John secretly wanted to laugh but tried to stay with him but security said he would have to go to Liverpool to try and get a same day passport, Russell turned to John "By the time I have done that you lot will be ready for coming back, apologise to Lindsay and Saron please John and I will see you when you all get back". John almost skipped down to the gate for departures.

Where's Russell everyone kept asking.,
John explained everything. "Typical
bloody Paddy!" "That's a bit harsh Bob"
replied John. "It might be but I bet you are
chuffed to little mint balls" he whispered
in Johns ear.

John smiled a smile that said it all.

They arrived in Rome and it was
scorching hot, the bus was waiting for
them, they checked into the hotel which
was stunning. "Done us proud here Linz"
Jimmy said, four bottles of beer on the bus
had made him a little bit merry.

"Ok everyone, check your rooms then let's
meet in reception in half an hour and go
and see what Rome has to offer shall
we?". They all agreed.

John was the first one down closely
followed by India, Tracey and Saron.

SMILE

Eventually they all arrived and headed in to the centre of Rome. Of course, the first thing was to find a bar. They all gave Shelley one hundred euros as a kitty, "Blimey Wez, that first round came to one hundred and eighteen euros!!" "Yep, not cheap here Shelley" "What if we go off the beaten track a bit and find a bar?" "Sounds good to me, I know one, it's called Angelo's, it's in the Jewish Ghetto". "Not sure about that, it sounds rough". "It's not Cheryl, it's what they call the area but it's beautiful, follow me you will love it"

John couldn't take his eyes of Saron, it was quite warm and she had a light blue mohair jumper that hung off one shoulder with a pair of skin tight brown leather trousers and a pale blue pair of kitten

heeled shoes, she complemented this with
a small necklace and a silver bangle on her
left arm. John was pretty sure Saron knew
he kept looking but she played it very
cool.

The Jewish Ghetto was stunning and the
architecture was breath- taking, they
wandered down the little cobbled streets
with beautiful flowers hanging over white
washed balconies, finally they arrived at
Angelo's, it was a medium sized bar and
restaurant with a big Italian man behind
the bar who turned out to be Angelo. "Ok
you lot, what are you all having?" almost
everyone except Bob and Jack went onto
the red wine, they took up all the stools at
the bar, Saron positioned herself between
Bob and John.

SMILE

"Isn't this lovely?" she said. "Yes, I'm impressed Saron, what do you think John?". John wasn't thinking about the lovely bar, he was thinking more about the lovely Saron and she knew it! Angelo was a great host and it was clear by 7.00pm that they were all in need of food, Angelo, sensing he would be losing them soon to a restaurant, brought out a massive lasagne with fresh salad. "This is on the house, as you say in England, you are all my friends, thank you for visiting me". "Cheers" said Shelley which created a Mexican wave from everyone at the bar except poor Cheryl who was by now the worse for wear. "I'd best take her back Wez". "Do you want me to come with you?" "No, I think I know my way mate, thank you though".

As the night went on they got louder and louder, Wez thought it best to say he would get everyone back to the hotel and those that wanted could have a beer in the hotel bar. With Bob gone some two hours ago Saron had moved up towards John, Tracey Rodgers kept looking over looking a bit miffed at the situation. They got off the bus and Wez said he was having a pint, Jack and Shelley said they would join him as did Tracey and India, the rest left for their rooms although Jimmy wanted a drink, Carol had a different idea. Luckily for John, Saron and his rooms were on the third floor, maybe Lindsay had planned this on purpose he thought. The rest got out at the second floor singing and generally being overloud. The lift doors closed. "What number are you?". Why

SMILE

Mister Gammon, are you propositioning me?"

John was a bit embarrassed so Saron played a long with it a bit more as the doors opened on the third floor. "Would you escort me to 317 please Mr Policeman". John by now was feeling this was going as planned, she used the key card and John followed her in.

Saron grabbed him and kissed him passionately, John was a bit taken aback at her intense petting, she suddenly pulled away, "Wait there Mr Policeman". John rang down to reception and ordered a bottle of champagne on room service, Saron was a long time and room service arrived, the little porter looked shocked as he handed over the ice bucket with the champagne. Saron came out of the bathroom in red lingerie with her beautiful blonde hair up and a pair of kitten heels slippers with a fur trim, similar to what you imagined Marilyn Monroe would have worn in her day.

The little porter left, John gave him a ten-euro tip. "Wow Saron, you look gorgeous". "I try my best Mr Gammon and champagne, you know how to spoil a lady" and she smiled that smile that just melted John.

They kissed and she fell on the bed, Saron was a very passionate person and everywhere John touched her she writhed in ecstasy. Saron closed her eyes and drifted into pure lust as her blonde hair, now loose, fell over her porcelain shoulders, her fingernails were scratching at John's back as he made love to her.

SMILE

John wanted this to last forever but her beauty and her alluring body meant it wasn't going to last, they both cried out in sheer passion both meeting their peak at the same time. John fell back on the bed. "I have missed you Mr Gammon". "Then pour me a glass of champagne" he said jokingly, Saron leaned over pouring a glass for them both.

"Why can't we commit to each other Saron? you could live with me and that way you are away from the pub as well for some time".

"John, it isn't me that can't commit, you know you have a problem with that, beside Mum would kill me I think" and she laughed with that infectious smile. "So, are you saying there is no chance we can ever be together?". "No, I'm not saying that but I saw how Tracey Rodgers was looking at you and I know you. Drink your champagne then cuddle me and let's enjoy Rome". "Ok sweetheart" and John kissed her again passionately.

The following day Saron said it was perhaps sensible to go to breakfast separately to save all the talk and especially Bob giving her and John grief. Saron went down first and John followed fifteen minutes later, Saron was sat with India and Tracey and John sat with Tony and Rita. "Ok everybody, today we are going to the Colosseum and the Trevi Fountain, possibly the greatest fountain to be found anywhere in the world". "Are you on commission Wez?" "Wish I was Carol" he replied.

SMILE

With breakfast done only Carol and
Jimmy decided to go off on their own,
Wez told them to be back at the bus by
9.00pm that night for the trip back to the
hotel.

They all followed Wez as he knew his way
to the Colosseum. This magnificent
building took their breath away and they
spent almost three hours wandering
around, John, as usual, couldn't take his
eyes off Saron, she seemed more
important than an old relic. Saron had
brown tight trousers cut just above the
ankle with a flat pair of cream coloured
shoes, she wore a cream coloured blouse
and a short brown leather jacket which she
was carrying because it was so hot. All
John could think about was spending the
night with her.

After the Colosseum the girls wanted to do
some shopping so the men found a small
bar and told them they would wait for
them there. Bob was only drinking coffee
he said he had an upset stomach, "More
like too much wine and ale last night old
lad". "Think you are right Jack" "I know I
am Tony!". "Yeah, Yeah, whatever you
two, put a sock in it".
The girls arrived back laden with
handbags and shoes etc. "Bloody hell how
much have you spent Cheryl?". "Just a bit
Bob". The rest of the guys were falling
about laughing, it then struck John that
Saron wasn't with them, how could he ask
without it being obvious? "I bet Saron
spent the most ladies". "Don't know, she
went in one shop and met a guy she was at
University with, he was Italian, a really

SMILE

good-looking guy, anyway, she said he
was going to take her out for dinner and
we haven't seen her since". John could
feel the jealousy rising up from the pit of
his stomach. Wez asked if they all wanted
to go and see the Trevi fountain or carry
on in this bar and see it Sunday, the bar
won the vote. As usual, the drinking took
on new heights and they all had a wobble
on going back to the bus including John,
who had been drowning his sorrows. They
arrived at the bus, Jimmy and Carol were
waiting as was Saron with a tall dark-
haired guy.
"Oh Antonio, these are my friends from
back home" and she introduce everyone,
when she got to John she just said, this is
John Gammon an old friend. She kissed

Antonio and said she would see him
tomorrow at 9.30 am at the hotel.
Back on the bus John was quiet and once
in the lift they hardly spoke, Saron just
said goodnight and went to her room
leaving John to go to his room by himself.

John lay on the bed checking his e mails
when his phone rang. "Hi John, its
Heather, nothing you can do and I don't
want to ruin your short break but Keri
Varney has been found dead with her face
cut like the others". "Did the surveillance
on Much bring up anything?" "Nothing
John, I feel we are getting nowhere fast".
"Do you want me to come back early?"
"No, don't be silly, Wally has to do his
forensic report, I will give you a call
tomorrow, I only wanted you to be kept in

SMILE

the loop. Hope you are having a lovely time in Rome, it's such a beautiful city". "Yes, it's lovely Heather, call me tomorrow". John hung up on the call. At least he had the latest murder to take his mind off Saron and the Italian Stallion. The following morning at breakfast Saron was a no show, Wez said she called him to say she was seeing the sites with Antonio so would see everyone the next day for the bus to the airport. John felt crest fallen and considered going back, making the murder of Keri Varney the excuse, eventually he made his mind up and got a taxi back to the airport and flew home.

Chapter 9

The following morning Heather was surprised to see John. "You didn't have to come back early John". "I know, I felt guilty enjoying a break knowing our killer has taken another life". He knew this wasn't the whole truth but he couldn't say he was jealous of Saron and the Italian.

At the meeting, Wally had some exciting news. "We know the victim is Keri Vaney, we also have DNA from who we think might be the assailant, the problem is, whoever it is isn't on our data base, she was quite badly beaten prior to her mouth being cut". "Ok, thanks Wally". "Yes Dave?" DI Smarty stood up. "We spoke with the guard that found her, it was the 11.05pm train from Manchester, he said when they reached Whaley Bridge there

SMILE

was only the lady in question on the train but he did state that there could have been somebody in the toilets". "Ok, DS Bass you get the CCTV for that night from Manchester and from all the stations to Bixton, I am looking for either Mulch or Belmont or anybody looking suspicious". "Ok sir". "I suggest ma'am that, once we have these results we bring Much and Belmont back and take their DNA, in my opinion it has to be one of these two". "Ok everybody, let's get to it". "Once DS Bass has the CCTV, DI Smarty, DI Lee and DI Milton help with the viewing please". Gammon went back to his office to catch up on the paperwork, grabbing a cup of coffee he sat at his desk still unable to get Saron out of his thoughts, is she tormenting me because of how I let her down at the wedding? His mind was everywhere and he knew he had to get his mind focused on the murders.

He had just finished one report when DCI Burns came in. "John, they are questioning my ability to solve these murders, they are talking of sending somebody called Claire Cassells, a serial killer specialist from Scotland Yard to sort it, do you know her?" "Yes, I know Claire, I worked with her many times, she is very capable".

"John, I feel the writing is on the wall for me". "Don't be silly, Claire goes to lots of forces if they are struggling".

"So, you think I am reading too much into it?" "Look, the reason I am here is because I came to help with a serial killer investigation many years ago and it was just circumstances that had me stopping.

SMILE

"Claire is a detective sergeant but she is being fast tracked, I will know tonight if she is coming". John didn't want to tell Heather the full story, he had an affair with Claire while he was in London and married to Lindsay. They had been going through a bad time and John was working on a case with Claire in Wiltshire and basically looked for solace with her, it wasn't long after that he was asked to come to the Peak District and basically he saw it has a way out. Claire was slim and had very striking looks and always had excellent dress sense.

Later that afternoon DCI Burns confirmed DS Cassells would be at Bixton for three weeks to help out, Heather said she was going to see Lisa Think that night to sort some accommodation for her.

The following day DS Bass and the rest of the team were trawling through the CCTV, Bass told Gammon they had not seen the face of either Much or Belmont but there had been three guys at different stops about the same build but wearing hoodies. "Ok Kate, show me". Bass brought up the first one at Stockport, he got on and got off at the next stop but Keri was still alive then and beside the train was full, the second guy, Gammon noticed a wedding ring which looked unusual, "Zoom in on that ring Kate". It was a silver ring with what looked like a blue or maybe purple inlay. "Does this guy get off?" "Well he got on at Whaley Bridge but after that we have no CCTV so he could have got off, the next CCTV we have is Bixton and he didn't get off there. There was no CCTV

SMILE

in the front carriage that Keri was in, the other guy is seen talking to this guy and they got off together at Furniss Vale so I think we can count those two out, that just leaves ring man". "Problem is sir, the Guard said the train was empty when he went through just after Chapel, he said there was only Keri in the front carriage, with there being no CCTV, and that is the only carriage without it, it was like he knew what he was doing".

"Damn right, get Belmont in for more questioning and a DNA test Kate, Dave you go with her, let me know when you get back, instruct DI Lee to get Belmont's solicitor here".

Gammon went back to his office and told DCI Burns what he knew so far. "Let's hope John, I really don't want us to look like we can't cope". "Don't panic Heather, its basic procedure, they did it with me when I was acting DCI, you know what this hierarchy are like, none of them understand policing, just take the help, it doesn't matter who find's the killer as long as the killings stop". "I suppose so John, I'm just so frightened of failing". "You won't fail, I'll see to that". "You are a kind man John Gammon" and she left his office.

It was almost 3.00pm when Belmont arrived, his solicitor was waiting in interview room one. Gammon instructed DS Bass to sort the recording and DI Smarty to help on the questioning.

"Good afternoon Craig". "Look Gammon, what the hell do you want now, who am I supposed to have murdered now?" "I'm

SMILE

unsure Craig, you tell me but your adversary Keri Vaney has been found murdered, so first things first, DI Smarty will take a swab test for your DNA". "Just a minute Mr Gammon, this is against my client's civil rights, he hasn't been charged with any crime". "Oh, if you want to play that game I can charge him right here right now if you wish?". The solicitor spoke with Belmont. "Ok he will take the DNA test but on the understanding that he is only doing this to prove his innocence". Gammon wondered how many times he had heard that over the years.

Smarty took the mouth swabs away for Wally to analyse. "So Craig, can you tell me your whereabouts on Saturday night". "Yes, I had been to see Manchester United play Tottenham Hotspur at Old Trafford, had a couple of beers in Manchester after the match then took the train to Bixton, only when I purchased my ticket, I only had enough money to get to Dove Holes, I left the train and walked back to Bixton to pick up my car from the train station".

"Could you show me your ring please?" Belmont showed Gammon his ring. "Most unusual Craig, is that Blue John?". "Yes, it's a promise ring, Lizzie bought it me a year or so ago".

Just the Smarty came back and asked Gammon to leave the room. "John, it's not Belmont's DNA". "Shit, I don't believe our luck Dave, that's him free again".

Gammon went back in the room. "You say you got off at Dove Holes and walked to Bixton did you see anybody?" "No, I know my way down the fields so unless

SMILE

you want to question some sheep and the odd cow perhaps". Belmont knew Gammon had nothing. "Ok Craig, we may need you for questioning as the cases =- progress, thanks for your time". Belmont smirked at Gammon as he left with his solicitor.

"That bloody man grates on me Dave". "Just another tosser John, we have them every day don't we?" "I guess we do mate". "So now what?" "I'm going to see DCI Burns, we need to get Much in". "Ok, let me know". Gammon stopped at Heather's office and explained he wanted Much bringing in. "Well I suppose now that Claire Cassells is coming we don't have anything to lose John".

Gammon told DI Smarty to get Much in for 11.00 am with his solicitor tomorrow,

John decided to head to the Tow'd Man because the Rome party would be back very soon in the Spinning Jenny and he wasn't sure he wanted to see Saron just yet.

At least DC was pleased to see him, she intertwined herself between his legs purring, "Ok DC, I know, I'm back early, now let's see what Phyllis has left me to eat DC. Wow, look at this, she made me a meat and potato pie and even a jug of gravy and some mash and peas, I don't know what we would do without Phyllis". John checked himself, here he was talking to cat which I'm sure she understood but was hardly going to answer him back! John warmed his dinner and poured a glass of bottled pedigree, by the time he had eaten and washed up it was 8.30pm so

SMILE

John decided to head to bed to read his book a thriller set in the afterlife "I Am Fawn Jones" It might give me inspiration he thought.

The following day he took the scenic route to Bixton up Dumpling Dale, it was a bright morning with the promise of a warm day. Gammon arrived at the station, PC Magic told him DCI Burns would like to see him in her office, Gammon climbed the stairs and knocked on her door. "Come in". Sat across from Heather was Claire Cassells, she hadn't aged at all, still the slim brown-haired girl with immaculate dress sense he remembered from his days in London.

"Hi Claire, how are you?". "Good thanks John, I'm staying at Cambridge Lodge, what a superb place". "Yes, its nice Claire and a nice couple running it, I like Lisa, she will make you very welcome". "So where do we start? DCI Burns has filled me in with the details, I believe you are having a suspect in today John?". "Yes Claire, sit in on the interview, here is the dossier on Graham Much, he will be here in about an hour".

"I'll leave you with it and will give you a shout when he arrives". Gammon left Claire with Heather reading about Much. It was 11.31 am when Magic said DI Smarty and DS Burns had Graham Much and his solicitor in interview room two. Gammon put his head round the door of Heather Burns's office. "Ok Claire, Much is here". She followed him down the old wooden staircase and into interview room two where DS Bass announced them to the

SMILE

tape. "Mr Gammon my client wishes to inform you that directly after this interview he will be speaking with the media as both myself and Mr Much feel it is totally out of order to keep this charade going on when Mr Much and his wife are grieving for their daughter Chelsea and the killer is out there".

"Your client is free to contact who he wishes but before he decides to do that he may want to listen long and hard to what I have to say".

"Graham Much, we believe that you are actually Malcolm Mulch, would we be correct in thinking that?" Much's solicitor looked a bit shocked and looked at Much. Much cleared his throat then quietly answered "Yes". "Mr Much could you please raise your voice for the tape please". "Yes, I was Malcolm Mulch". "Why did you change your name Mr Much?" "Never liked Malcolm or Mulch so I changed it to Graham Much". "Really? It wasn't perhaps to do with your incarceration was it Mr Much? In fact, you served twelve years because of sexual indiscretions is that correct? I believe, girls in their late teens or early twenties, do you see where I am going with this Mr Much?"

"I served my time, changed my name and met Lorna, she knows nothing of my past". "So, Chelsea wasn't your daughter then Graham?" Again, Much cleared his throat in a nervous manner. "No, she is my step daughter". "She was a pretty girl wasn't she Graham did you make advances to her and she knocked you

SMILE

back?" "No, no I didn't, I am happy with Lorna, that is in my past". "Well you have to see it from our point of view Graham, we have a man who reports his daughter, or so he tells us at the time, is missing blaming a boyfriend. Lorna Much has no idea that she is living with a convicted sex offender who likes young girls, so isn't it time we had some honesty Graham? because from where I am sitting this isn't good". "I have done nothing wrong, won't you people ever let me have a life?" "You said in a statement that you supported Chelsea football club hence the name Chelsea for who you said was your daughter yet she was not your daughter and must have been about thirteen when you met Lorna so was that another lie Graham?" "No, when I first met Lorna she was sat next to me for a cup game at Stamford Bridge, we got talking and although she said she didn't get to many games since she was divorced because money was tight a friend had given her the cup ticket, it was then she told me she had called her daughter Chelsea".

"Do you know Graham, I am going to hold you for twenty-four hours while we do a search on your house and vehicle, do you own any other properties?" Much was quiet for a minute but then said he had a shed on an allotment down Green Lane in Dilley Dale. "Ok, DI Smarty will get you booked into the holding cell and we will speak tomorrow". Gammon turned to the solicitor "Please be here for 1.30pm tomorrow and we will carry on this interview".

SMILE

They left the room and John sat with Claire Cassells. "John, the latest murder of the young girl Keri Vaney, who questioned the Guard who reported her dead and what time was it called in?" "I'm not sure Claire, I was actually on a short break in Rome when Heather Burns contacted me".

"Ok I will speak with Heather". "What are you thinking?" "Nothing yet, I just want to get my ducks in a row". John knew Claire, she played her cards close to her chest but he also knew she would dig and dig and he just hoped Heather had followed some kind of procedure.

He decided to ask Magic for the call- in log, with Keri Vaney dead he had no witness to her attack in Dumpling Dale, if it was indeed Craig Belmont. Something wasn't stacking up. "The call came in at 12.10 am sir from a Kevin Travis, he was the guard that found her on the Manchester train". "What time does the Manchester train get into Bixton?". "Just a minute sir" and PC Magic looked it up it, "It should arrive at 11.44pm" "Ok Magic, who was the officer who interviewed Kevin Travis?" "DI Finney sir". "Ok, thanks Magic, is Finney in?" "Yes sir, he shares an office with DI Stampfer". Gammon climbed the stairs, Claire had alerted him to something. "DI Stampfer can you leave me and DI Finney for a moment please?". "Sure can" he said. "DI Finney, you were the DI on the scene at Bixton where Keri Vaney was murdered in the front carriage is that correct?". "Yes, I arrived at 12.40am with Wally and the

SMILE

team". "Ok, when you questioned the guard, a Mr Kevin Travis, how did he say he found Keri?". "He said she had been beaten quite badly, in his notes he said her dress was ripped as if some sort of sexual behaviour had gone on". "Did Wally confirm anything?" "We haven't had anything from Wally?" "What? Have you asked for it DI Finney? "No Sir because it's pretty obvious that it's our serial killer". "Bloody hell man, I thought all this had been put to bed, don't ever assume again" and Gammon stormed out. He went straight down to Wally's office. "Hi John". "Hi Wally, Keri Vaney, any sign of sexual misbehaviour?" "Yes, she had been sexually assaulted, I informed DCI Burns". "Shit, I leave them for a few days and look what a bloody mess we are in, Ok thanks Wally". Next John headed to see DCI Burns, as he entered her office Claire was coming out, "I am going to bring Kevin Travis, the guard in John, somethings not right here, the time delay from her being supposedly found to the time he called in to Bixton station, it's all wrong. Keri Vaney wasn't cut like the other girls, she only had one side of her mouth cut, I'll give you a call when I get him back here".

DS Cassells left the office and DCI Burns knew she had cocked up. "Heather this is bad, I wrongly assumed she was a victim of our serial killer, it looks like she wasn't, Wally said she was sexually attacked, the guard was very late calling the murder in, it's a bloody catalogue of errors and Claire found it straight away".

SMILE

"John look, it's my fault, I was tired when I got the call and wasn't thinking in any depth". "Whichever way, this looks bad for both of us Heather, if Claire chooses to report this, and I have no doubt she will, she plays everything by the rules then there will be questions asked"

A couple of hours passed, when Travis arrived with his solicitor they put him in interview room one. DS Cassells, Di Gammon and DS Bass was in charge of the recording. "I am Mich Duffy, Kevin's solicitor, now what is this all about?" "Well Kevin" said Gammon, totally ignoring the jumped-up Duffy "I would like to get one of my officers to do a swab test with you for DNA". "My client hasn't been incriminated in any crime". "Then

you won't mind Kevin, that way we can
eliminate you from our enquires".
Gammon called Stella Broom one of
Wally's staff, she took the sample away.
"Ok, so Kevin, you are ok if I call you
Kevin?" "Yes". "I would like you to run
through what happened from leaving
Manchester Piccadilly to you finding the
body of Keri Vaney and consequently
calling Bixton police to report it".
"Well, as usual, my first job is to ensure
all passengers have tickets". "And you do
this how?" "My system is, I try and get
down all the carriages before any stops
then I watch who is getting on at the
various stops and ask them for their
ticket".
"Ok Kevin thanks, did Keri Vaney have a
ticket?". He thought for a second then

SMILE

replied yes. "So, you were happy she was a paying customer". "Yes, I was". "Did you see anyone talking to Keri?" "I didn't notice but I wasn't particularly looking". "Did you see this man?" Gammon pushed a picture of Belmont toward Travis. "Have you ever seen this man before?" "Yes, he was on the train that night". "Which carriage?" "Carriage five, I remember him because he said he needed to get to Bixton but his ticket was only paid to get to Dove Holes and I made him leave the train there, he shouted "jobs worth" at me and stuck one finger in the air as he left" "So at no time did you see Keri Vaney, the victim, talk to this man?". "No, I am sure". "Ok Kevin, we are doing great, now you called Bixton station at 12.10 am to say you had found the body later identified as

Keri Vaney, is that correct?". Travis hesitated. "If you say that's what the time was, I really don't know".

Gammon now played an ace card, he wasn't sure if it would work but he sensed he had Travis on the ropes. "So, the time of death for Keri Vaney was put at 11.44am or thereabouts yet you didn't contact anybody until twenty-four minutes later did you Kevin?" "I told you I don't know what time I rang, I was in shock". "I would like that noting on the report that my client was in dreadful shock when he called Bixton police".

Stella came back with the DNA result she pulled Gammon outside. "Sir, John Walvin said to tell you they found semen on Keri Vaney's clothes and it is a match to the DNA I took". Gammon could have

SMILE

hugged, her this was the break- through he wanted.

Gammon went back in the room and DS Bass started the tape again. "Ok Kevin, there are no records of Keri Vaney purchasing a ticket either on line or at the station so I am going to put a scenario to you, I would say you suggested that Keri Vaney could pay for the ride to Bixton in kind or you were calling transport police". "No that's rubbish". "Kevin, I am giving you a chance to make your sentence lighter. I believe you killed Keri Vaney, I'm not sure if it was intentional but I am pretty sure you killed her, we know you had some kind of sexual agreement with her because we found semen on Keri's body and your DNA proves it was yours"

At that point Travis broke down. "I didn't mean to kill her, she wanted me to strangle her, she said she got some kind of kick from it while she was satisfying me, she choked Mr Gammon, I didn't know what to do, there was just me and her on the train. I always let George pull in the train on a Saturday then he goes straight away, he likes a drink at his Legion club so I lock everything up".

"Kevin Travis, I am charging you with the murder of Keri Vaney, you do not have to say anything but what you do say will be taken down and may be used in evidence, are we clear?". Travis nodded. "Take him down to the holding cells please DS Bass?".

Duffy, Travis solicitor, wasn't so smug now as he left the station. "John have you

SMILE

got a minute? Good police work but I do have concerns over DCI Burns, she should have been on top of this while you were away I mean, she is a DCI !!" "Claire I'm not asking you to bend any rules but we all make mistakes, she is under a lot of pressure at the minute as you know with them sending you to help out" "So what are you saying John?". I'm saying let the station celebrate tonight, we have one case put to bed". "Ok, I wouldn't do this for anyone else John". "Thanks Claire". Gammon went straight to Heather and told her about Travis and what Claire Cassells had said. "I can't thank you enough John". "Hey, forget about it, I have made my share of mistakes. Let's book the Spinning Jenny tonight for the station, its tradition when we have a big result". "Ok John but

I can't stop long tonight". "Well even if
you show your face you will be fine".
Gammon rang Wez and asked him to put
some sandwiches and chilli etc on for
them and he would pay for it, he said they
would be there about 5.30pm.
Gammon carried on wading through his
paperwork, all the time believing that
Graham Much was the man for the
murders, his background was leading him
that way.
It was soon 5.30pm and the Spinning
Jenny was full, Wez had done John proud,
there were Sandwiches a curry, chilli, and
a cottage pie, for once the whole station
had turned out which was pleasing, it
showed moral was good he told Heather.
Tracey Rodgers wandered over to John,
she said Wez had asked her if it got too

SMILE

busy would she help out in the bar but at the moment they were coping. "So, Rome was a flop for you then John?". "No, I enjoyed what time I had". "I remember you had to leave Barcelona early for work, you need to get a different job" and she laughed.

"Mr Gammon" "Hey Sheba, how are you?" "Yeah good, not heard from you in a while, you ok?". "Just so much on at work Sheba". "I hear you had to leave the Rome trip early because of work". "Goes with the territory I'm afraid, this food Wez has put on is great". "Yes, he does a good job and to be fair I didn't give him much notice".

It was now almost 9.00pm and there weren't many of the police left, John was stood with Kev and Doreen and Tony and

Rita and then there was just a few locals about, finishing off the free food.

"So John, how's the love life since we came out of the pub? we have been that busy we have hardly been in, last I heard you were seeing Sheba Filey". I'm not really seeing anyone". "We heard Saron actually met a guy in Rome, bit of a looker mate!" "Kevin stop winding John up".

"I'm not Doreen, honest" and he laughed but it didn't seem to have the same effect now that he doesn't wear his trademark dickie bow.

John always enjoyed Kev's, company they had been friends for many years and he was always the voice of reason with John. "Right you two, I'm off, got a cat to see". "A cat John?" "Yeah, Saron bought me a white cat which she called dark chocolate

SMILE

which has been shortened to DC of course, she is great company Doreen". "Well at least that lady won't get you into any trouble" she said laughing. "We will see you sweetheart" "Bye" and John left telling Wez he would settle with him for the food next time he was in.

DC was sat by the fire Phyllis had made and wasn't keen to leave it but she did reluctantly and John stroked her. "Well DC, one case cracked now just the big one". DC wasn't interested and headed to her place next to the log burner.

Dave Smarty had told John that when he went to see Keri Vaney's grandma, Monica James, to tell her the news she didn't seem upset. John at first thought she had probably had enough of her granddaughter's way's but the more he thought about it the more it left him intrigued, he decided the next day he would go and see Monica James to see what reaction he got.

The following morning John called DCI Burns and said he was going to Dilley Dale to have a chat with Keri Vaney's grandma, Burns said DS Cassells was questioning everybody on the suspects they had, John explained this was normal from Claire and she was to stop being paranoid.

Gammon set off for Dilley Dale, he thought about dropping in for a coffee with Jeannetta Goslyarnee but he would have to see what time he had. Gammon pulled up at Crowstones House in Dilley Dale, Monica James was just about to

SMILE

leave. "Mrs James". "Oh, hello Mr Gammon". "I wondered if I could have five minutes of your time?". "Of course, I was just popping to the post office for my pension do come in, would you like a cup of tea?". "That would be very nice thank you, I just thought I would pop by, I was away when you were informed about Keri". "Yes, a lovely man, Mr Smarty, he came and told me" "Please don't take this the wrong way but he thought you were in shock at the news". "No I wasn't Mr Gammon, Keri the beautiful girl was lost when her mother and father passed away, she was never the same. I had been quite ill over the years with the worry caused by Keri so much so that my sister in law Marion said I needed to give her space, they have a son a bit older than Keri and

he is a bit wild, you know tattoos, ear
rings and studs everywhere and they said
he will grow out of it, he has a flat in
Micklock and lives with a girl now".
"What's your nephew called?" "Peter
Krass, I tried to follow that advice with
Keri but I guess deep down I knew she
was always going to end up in a bad way
Mr Gammon, it was like it was her
destiny". Gammon decided not to mention
that Mr and Mrs Murray had contacted the
police to say their daughter was missing,
he was guessing they hadn't told Monica
James believing she had enough on her
plate with Keri.
"Ok Monica, as long as you are ok I will
bid you farewell". "Well thank you for
coming to see me, it was very good of you
Mr Gammon". "Do you need a lift to the

post office for your pension Monica?"
"No, I'm fine, I need the exercise but
thank you".

Gammon drove back to Bixton thinking
about the connection between Krass and
Keri Vaney, as soon as he got back he
shared his findings with DS Cassells and
DCI Burns.

DS Cassells felt she would like to question
Graham Much, she felt she could get him
to crack, both John and Heather thought it
best to leave him alone at the minute or
the next thing would a charge of police
harassment against them unless they had
something really concrete.

Gammon could see that DS Cassells
wasn't happy at the negativity shown by
Gammon and Burns so she left the office.
"Be ready for a call Heather, DS Cassells

is used to getting her own way and she will feel we are stopping her doing her job". "That's rubbish John but at the moment it's quite useless unless we have something new".

Gammon left the office trying to think if there could be any connection between Krass and his cousin Keri Vaney, nothing was making Gammon think there could be any tie up to the other murders.

It was almost 6.00pm when Gammon left work and headed to pay the food bill at the Spinning Jenny, it was a bit embarrassing for John as Laura Slooter was behind the bar but she was fine, she had realised she was too young for John and knew John felt bad so there was no mention. She poured John a pint of Pedigree. "Is Wez in?"

"They have gone out for a meal John, I

SMILE

think it's their wedding anniversary, they said they will be back at 8.30pm. John decided to hang on, he didn't like owing money and Wez had made such a good job of the food. The pub was quite busy and Lindsay and Wez arrived back at 8.40pm. "Let me get you two a drink for your wedding anniversary". "Very good of you John, I'll have a white wine spritzer" "and a pint of Stella for me John please". "What do I owe you for last night mate?" "Call it eighty pounds John". "No way, it must have cost you that to put it on, I'll give you one hundred and forty is that ok?" "More than ok John, thanks". "So where did you go for your meal?" "Churchtown Manor". "Was it good?" "Excellent John but the poor lady that owns it, Christina, she looked dreadful, she was putting a brave face on things but the fact her daughter was murdered must have really knocked the stuffing out of her". "I really can't imagine Wez, I'm sure we will get the killer, it's only a matter of time but that isn't a consolation to the poor families this maniac hurts with his or her actions" "John let's get on to a different subject". "You are right Lindsay, so how long have you two been married?" "Ten years John", Lindsay tapped Wez playfully, "He is useless, its eleven years". "Just testing". "I believe you Wez!". "Thanks John, shame you missed the last day in Rome John, we went to the Vatican and some other sites". "I was enjoying it mate but things went a bit wrong here so thought I best cut it short".

SMILE

"Saron is good fun isn't she John?". "Yes, a barrel full of laughs Lindsay". "Do I detect some annoyance there my friend?" "No nothing new Wez". "That guy she met, the Italian who she knew from her college days was just a friend John, they met up with us and he left at 8.00pm nothing going on, shall we move on Linz?" "Ha ha, nice one, just trying to help us women see everything John".

"Sure you do" and he laughed. "Well Wez said our next trip is a bowling night, do you bowl John?" "Kind of". John didn't want to tell them he was the under eleven North Derbyshire bowling champion, it just sounded a bit big headed. "So, would you be up for a game or two?". "When are you thinking Wez?" "One Friday night say in a couple of weeks?". "Ok mate, put me down for that". "You will need a partner, I thought we could have mixed teams". "Ok I'll think of somebody". "I bet you do John Gammon" came a voice over his left shoulder. "Hey Shelley, how are you?" "Good John". "What are you drinking?" "Can I have a Prosecco?" "No problem, what about Jack?" "I'll have a brandy mate, got a bit of an upset stomach at the minute".

John ordered the drinks which duly arrived. "So, are you coming bowling John?" "Yeah, I just told Wez I was up for that" "Ok then Mr Gammon, who is your partner?". "Not thought about it Shelley". "Ok, well I will think for you, I am playing badminton with Cheryl and Sheba tomorrow, shall I tell her you asked me to ask her?". "Yes, that would be great".

SMILE

"Right well that's sorted". "Women hey John, we don't have a say but nice choice mate". "I heard that Jack Etchings" and Shelley playfully tapped him on his head making Jack laugh.

John was enjoying the evening when his phone rang. "Excuse me, I have to take this, its work" and he wandered into a corner. "Hello?". "Hi John, Dave Smarty here, just had a call from PC Magic, two guys out on mountain bikes saw a man fleeing a scene, when they got close a young girl was bleeding to death, they tried to save her but no luck, I have sent Wally over to Micklock Moor and I am on my way now". "Ok Dave, I am on my way. Sorry folks, duty calls". "I'll tell Sheba" Shelley said as John rushed out. This all we need John thought on his way, poor Heather is under enough pressure. John parked his car and walked to the Stepping Stones, a beautiful part of Micklock Moor which back in the day would have had a fantastic view, Gammon could see Wally's white tent flapping in the wind as he approached, as he got closer he could see Smarty and he thought DI Milton talking to two guys with bikes, Gammon flashed his badge to the two men. "Tell me, what did you see?" "We were coming over Clover Edge and we saw a guy running across the field in front of the Stepping Stones well, I saw a guy, it could have been a woman it was dark and hard to tell, when we got closer we saw the girl, she was bleeding profusely from her mouth wounds, I told my friend to shine the torch on her, I tried desperately

SMILE

to stem the blood but it was too late. she must have lost so much, she just went limp in my arms". "Did she say anything?" She tried but her mouth was so bad she was incoherent". "Ok lads, my officers will take your names and addresses and we will be in touch if we need to talk again" Gammon wandered over to Wally who made his usual comment about policeman plod fowling his crime scene. "What have you got mate?" "Very little at the moment John, she is somewhere between eighteen and twenty-two, I would say she is of mixed parentage and she bled to death, other than that you will have to wait until the morning where I suppose you want a full report by 9.00 am". "Thanks mate, you know me well"

Gammon told Smarty and Milton to call it
a night and that they would meet in the
morning at 9.00 am when hopefully Wally
would have more for them.
John drove home feeling somewhat
inadequate, that was another murder and
they were nowhere nearer finding the
killer, he knew the hierarchy would not
allow this to go on much longer.
He pulled into the farmyard which was
pitch black, other than his light over his
front door. He entered the kitchen and
little DC scampered to him. Saron hadn't
been wrong when she said DC would be
great company, she was intertwined
between his legs looking so pleased to see
him.
"Well DC it's been a long day so I'm off
to bed, you coming?" DC's tail went bolt

SMILE

upright and she scampered up the stairs
determined to be on the bed before John.

Chapter 10

The following day he set off for Bixton taking his favourite route through Dumpling Dale, there were new born lambs everywhere, which was a sign Pritwich sheep races would be taking place soon.

Gammon arrived at Bixton and had a quick word with PC Magic who said everything had been quiet on the night shift, other than that DS Cassells had arrived at work at 4.00 am, this concerned Gammon, that meant Claire was onto something, he knew her from old, she was like a dog with a bone once she found a trail, he decided to put his head around her door. "Morning Claire everything ok?" "Yes, all good John, just working on a few theories". "Well if you get anything let me

SMILE

know in case we are working on the same thing, don't forget the meeting at 9.00am in the incident room". "No fear of that John".

Gammon went straight to his office, grabbing a coffee on the way. He stood looking at Losehill bathed in beautiful sunlight, possibly one of his favourite views anywhere in the world. Spot on 9.00am Gammon made his way to the incident room.

"Ok everybody, settle down, first thing up, Wally, do we have a positive identification on the latest victim?". "Yes, her name is Chloe Fammargia Murray, a girl aged about seventeen of mixed race, there was no sexual assault on the victim, she died from bleeding to death with the customary slashing of both sides of her mouth. Like the others she would have been in tremendous pain had she not been sedated" "Wally, like the others, was she killed where she was found?! "No, I don't think so, everything points to her being placed at the scene".

DI Smarty, just run through what the two cyclists told you". "One of the men tried to stem the bleeding but to no avail the other stated that a long way in the distance they did see somebody running they were unsure if that person was male or female".

"Thanks Dave, Ok, it may be that our killer was almost caught in the act which means he or she is getting sloppy, we have a few suspects, DI Smarty and DI Lee you go and question where Graham Much was last night, Finney and Stampfer, you check out Craig Belmont, DS Bass and DI

SMILE

Milton I would like you to speak with Paul
Krass, DS Yap and myself will speak with
Raznak Bolan who I believe is over here
for a board meeting at "In The Buff Model
Agency" If any of you find they don't
have an alibi then I want to know, ok,
thanks everybody".

Claire pulled John aside. "John, I don't
think any of these people are your killers, I
have profiled them and they don't fit the
rules". "Well Claire, rules are made to be
broken. Could you go and break the sad
news of their daughter to Mr and Mrs
Murray please? Come on DS Yap, you are
driving". He left Claire Cassells open
mouthed as he dismissed her.

"Seemed a bit harsh sir with DS Cassells".
"I know her well and if you give her an
inch she will take a yard, trust me on this".

Yap pulled into the old market square in Ackbourne, "Come on Yap, I will treat you to a breakfast before we go and see Bolan".

Andrea's Little Tea Pot had stood for over two hundred years in the same place, the lady that ran it now was sixth generation, John's mum used to love calling at the café with Phil on their shopping day on a Thursday.

It was a quaint little tea room with eight tables of four and two tables of two, they grabbed the two in the window. A pleasant lady in her mid- fifties came with a menu. "Would you like a drink?" "A strong black coffee please". "A tea for me" Milk and sugar?" "Oh, yes please". "Sugar? now that's not good for you Ian". "Neither is watching Derby County week in and week

SMILE

out sir but I still do it!" "Good point" said
Gammon and laughed. They ordered a
breakfast with Derbyshire oatcakes, when
they had finished Yap turned to Gammon
and said, "that must be the best breakfast I
have ever had sir, thank you" "Not a
problem, Ian let me pay and we can be on
our way".

It was 11.00am when they arrived at the
Agency, Sandra Cullen was at reception.
"Mr Gammon how can I help you?" "Well
I remembered you said you had a board
meeting today and that Raznak Bolan
would be over for it so I wondered if we
could have a word with him". "I'm sorry,
it's been put off for a month, Raznak had
other commitments come up". Crap, John
thought. "Ok Sandra, just a quick
question, all these murders how are they

affecting your business?" "Hardly at all Mr Gammon, very sad for the parents of these girls and the latest one was Chloe, only seventeen so, we hadn't taken her on" "How did you know Chloe was dead?" "Her father rang about thirty minutes ago" "Oh, why would he ring you?" Well Chloe would have been eighteen in about two and a half months and I had promised her a contract, she was a very pretty girl so I guess he just wanted to let me know".

"Ok Sandra but I do wish to speak to Mr Bolan so if you could let him know please, if he is coming to the UK before your next meeting I do wish him to get in contact" "Ok Mr Gammon, I will pass the message on".

Gammon and Yap left the Agency and walked the cobbled streets of Ackbourne

SMILE

back to the car. "That struck me as odd that Brian Murray should call Sandra Cullen so soon after DS Cassells must have broken the news". "I smell a rat DS Yap". "Think you could be right, I wonder if Murray and Sandra Cullen were having an affair?" "When you get back and DS Bass is back, check Murray's bank account for hotels, flowers anything that might mean he was seeing Cullen". "Ok sir".

Back at the station, all the officers Gammon had sent to speak to the suspects had alibis for the previous night. He told DS Cassells of his suspicion of Murray and Cullen, she dismissed his judgement clearly still upset with Gammon's brusque nature towards her earlier.

DS Bass set about Murray's bank accounts, she wasn't long finding what Gammon had thought. "Sir, he has four bank accounts, one shared with his wife, one savings account, one building society account and a separate bank account and that one makes for some great reading. He sends flower from a company called Crystal flowers in Ackbourne, same cost every week to, guess where? Sandra Cullen, Witch Tor Road, Osmenton, I looked up this address and it is owned by a Brian Murray, apparently it stands empty but it looks like he meets Cullen there every Thursday and the flowers are always delivered to the same place, a small former coal shed attached to the property. I would guess he leaves a key in there sir then she sees the flowers every week, also, about

SMILE

every two months he goes to Whitby to the
Palace Hotel for one night, no doubt that
you are correct sir". "Ok Kate, great work,
now we have to figure what involvement,
if any, they have in these murders and if so
why would Brian Murray kill his own
daughter? Ok Kate, keep this to yourself, I
need to think this through before taking
any action". The following day Gammon
had decided to have a go at Brian Murray,
he told DS Bass to bring him in for some
questioning but not to spook him or his
wife because they had only just lost Chloe.
Murray arrived and Bass took him into
interview room two, Gammon joined her.
"Mr Murray, am I ok to call you Brian?".
"Yes of course, is this about our Chloe?"
"Well, kind of Brian, you see yesterday
we were at the model agency and Sandra

Cullen said you had called her to tell her about Chloe is that correct?". "Yes it was Mr Gammon, she had been very good with Chloe". "Ok Brian so there was no other reason to contact Sandra Cullen?". "No, why would there be?". "Well you see, that got me thinking so I did a bit of digging, do you own a house in Osmenton?" "Why are you asking me these questions? I thought I was coming to help you". "Well hopefully you will be able to Brian". "Yes I do own a house, I am going to do it up". "Have you heard of a company called Crystal Flowers in Ackbourne?" Murray hesitated. "Look what is this?" "Just answer the question Brian". "Ok, yes I do actually". "Do you have a bouquet of flowers delivered to the address in Osmenton every Thursday by Crystal

SMILE

Flowers?" "Look, I think I want a solicitor present, this is private business". "Brian, we can make this as hard or as easy as you wish, the hard way is we wait a couple of days and we bring you in officially then almost certainly your wife will know about the affair with Sandra Cullen, which is it to be?"

"Ok, Sandra and I are seeing each other and have been for six months, we meet every Thursday at the house. What you see with me and my wife isn't reality you see, when I worked on the island where I met Tamisha she was already pregnant with Chloe, Chloe is not my daughter. Tamisha had been seeing a very tasty character that virtually ran the island, she told me he beat her often and was insanely jealous, my contract only had a few weeks to go so

we hatched a plan to get her off the island
and away from him. It was on the sea
crossing that she told me that she was
pregnant but not by the guy she was
running away from but a guy by the name
of Paul Paulson who was an aid worker on
the island, she said he didn't know.
I wrongly assumed that she wanted me
but, if I am honest, I was punching way
above my weight with Tamisha, she just
wanted residency in the UK and marrying
me gave her that. We had an ok marriage
at first but looking back that was just a
charade, she didn't want deporting back or
she knew she would face certain death.
After eleven years she said she could no
longer bear me touching her but wanted to
stay together for Chloe as she was
innocent in all this. I had a few girlfriends,

SMILE

discreetly of course and then I met Sandra. You are right Tamisha doesn't know about Sandra or the cottage, she would see that as dreadful, knowing the woman I was sleeping with. This all sounds bad but Tamisha isn't a bad person, yes she used me but who wouldn't have been besotted by her and her looks and figure Mr Gammon?"

"So you and Chloe did get on?" "Well we had our ups and downs but what parents don't have at some point as their kids become teenagers?" "Ok Mr Murray, thank you for your time and the explanation, I think we can conclude this chat". Murray left the station.

Gammon met Claire on the stairs, "How did you get on with Murray?" "It's a long story but pretty sure we can strike him off the suspect list". "I don't want to say I told you John!" and she skipped past him. What was wrong with Claire? he felt he had severely stood on her toes and he was pretty sure it was because of DCI Burns and him asking her not to report, Claire was the consummate professional and she would not have been happy with that. With nothing further on the case, he was beginning to get quite concerned. In need of some TLC he decided to chance a call to Saron as he drove away from work. "Hi John". Saron sounded very bubbly, "how are you?" "Oh ok, just a bit fed up with work and could do with cheering up, are you working tonight?" "Actually I'm not, Russell asked me if I would like to go ice skating then a meal in Derby". "Oh, ok, perhaps speak later" and John hung up.

SMILE

That conversation just about summed John's life up at present. He headed for the Spinning Jenny with just one thing on his mind, to get as drunk as he could and obliterate the conversation he had just had with Saron.

Wez was working the bar and there was a party of about six in wearing walking boots and that was it, but it was only 6.10pm. "I'll have a Pedigree and a brandy chaser please mate and one for you". "Thanks, are you on a bender tonight?" "Hopefully!". Wez thought it best not to ask anymore. John downed the brandy and ordered another one, this went on for the first hour and John was a little tipsy by the time Kev and Doreen came in. "Hey my best mate and his utterly gorgeous wife, what are you drinking?". "Flattery will get

you everywhere, I'll have a large vodka and coke, what about you Kev?"
"Pedigree please, are you ok?" "Never been better" he said in a slurred tone.
"Wez get my mate a double Brandy as well"
"So what you doing in here on your own?"
"Well I'm guessing he had a date and she didn't show". "Are you losing your grip John?" "Well actually Doreen is half right, I was going to ask Saron out for a meal tonight but she is going out with that Paddy ice skating". "Oh John Gammon, she is giving you the run around, I've never seen you like this" and Doreen pecked him on the cheek. "It's time you bloody settled down, out playing the field you will never be happy John".

SMILE

He smiled as he downed another brandy then insisted on buying the rest of the bottle to share with Kev. By 11.00pm John was so out of it Doreen asked Wez if he had a room for him for the night, she took him to bed like she had done many times over the years then got Kev home who wasn't as bad but he was bad enough. The following day Lindsay did John a full English breakfast, she said her dad always said it cured a hangover. He ate it but more out of politeness than anything else because he felt so rough. It was almost 10.00 am before he decided to drive, he thanked Lindsay and Wez for their kindness and set off up the steps to the car park, just then his phone rang, he realised he had left it in the glove compartment of the car. "John, where are you?". "Sorry mate, I feel a bit rough, I'm just about to set off from the Spinning Jenny". "Stop where you are, I'll come and get you, we have just had a report in from Shealdon, it looks like our killer struck again, I was on my way but I'll pick you up on the way through mate, I'm only five minutes away". "Thanks Dave". He sat in his car feeling dreadful and stupid at the same time.

Smarty arrived, "Get in mate, landlady from the Broken Egg was walking her dog when she came across a young girl bleeding to death". "Ok mate, enough of the grim details, I will throw up if I hear anymore". "Blimey you must have really hit it hard last night, that isn't like you". Gammon sat quiet until they finally arrived in the village of Shealdon, two

SMILE

fields up from the Broken Egg Gammon could see Wally's forensic tent, he also saw the landlady from the Broken Egg walking down towards the pub. "Excuse me, are you the lady that rang in about the young girl?" "Yes". "I'm DI Gammon and this is DI Smarty". "I was walking my dog when I found her so I phoned you lot". It sounded a bit dismissive but that was the way she was, say it as it is John thought. "Come in the pub and I will explain". "Ok, could I have your name please?". "It's Claire Bright, I'm the landlady here at the Broken Egg, I always take Poacher my German shepherd up the fields about 8.00 am every morning, Poacher never runs off but this morning he scampered of so I was bloody mad at him, that was until I saw he had found the girl and was sat with her as

if he was guarding her Mr Gammon".
"Was she alive when you got there?" "No,
I felt for a pulse, I was a nurse until I took
the pub on so would have known what to
do but she was dead, there was a lot of
blood" "Ok Claire, well we know where
you are if we need you"
"Never mind that, come and have one of
our incredible lamb dinners, you coppers
are on mega money, spend a bit with me"
and she laughed. "Sparky lady" "She
certainly is Dave". They headed up the
fields to Wally, by now with the wind
blowing John was feeling a shade better.
"Morning Wally, what have we got?"
"Same thing, bled to death, both sides of
her mouth cut, young girl, I would say
maybe eighteen to twenty". "Any sexual
contact?" "Blimey John, give us chance,

SMILE

I'll have all that information for you in the morning". "Ok mate, 9.00am?". "Ok, slave driver." "Dave, take me back for my car then we'd best get into work". "Ok not a problem". They eventually arrived at Bixton at 1.30pm, Gammon went straight to Heather Burns and explained what had happened. Smarty told PC Magic to get the team together in the incident room for 9.00 am in the morning.

"Another body then John? I think it's time we sat down and I discuss my theory with you". "By all means, let's get a coffee" they sat in Gammon's office. "Out of all the people you have as suspects, just run through their jobs".

Gammon looked puzzled but started.

"Graham Much, bricklayer, Craig Belmont, former photographer now stacks shelves at Morrison's in Bixton, Glyn Doolan, lives in sheltered accommodation, he found one of the bodies, he said he was out checking his rabbit traps, he did have a knife on him which he was very handy at skinning rabbits with, the knife showed no evidence it was used in the crime. I did consider Brian Murray until yesterday and after questioning him I do believe we can discount him. I have yet to question Raznak Bolan who is a director at In the Buff Model Agency". "What are your thoughts on him?" "Well, all the girls had some tie up with this agency and I wondered initially about human trafficking but I really don't know. These are the main suspects Claire, now what are you thinking?". "My feeling is it could be a local Park Ranger or somebody interested

SMILE

in the local area. The places these girls were found, why would you bother to drag them to these places? it doesn't make sense".

"So what do we look for?" "A male, maybe thirty to forty, lives on his own maybe shy but maybe not, knows the area well and I believe this person is holding a grudge and that could be against the police or maybe one of these girls, I don't think it's all of them, I think most of the killings are a smoke screen". "Ok Claire, so now what?" "Well this is where you come in, who do you know that might fit that description?" "I don't think I actually do know anybody but I will ask about, discreetly of course".

The following day at the meeting Gammon got a big shock when Wally got up to give his informed opinion on the body found. "Ok Wally, what do you have for us?" "She was a white female aged somewhere between eighteen and twenty-five, she had been sexually assaulted unlike the others, but she still had her mouth cut both sides. From dental records her name is Laura Slooter and the address in her handbag is The Spinning Jenny". Gammon was mortified, he kept his composure. "Anything else Wally?" "Her hand bag was intact, it doesn't look like the killer had taken anything".

"Ok thanks, well it just gets worse, this girl started working at the Spinning Jenny as a barmaid, we'd best go and do some digging, DI Smarty you come with me, DS Bass and DI Milton, the usual bank

SMILE

account checks please, we are looking for something unusual".

"John before you go can I have a word?".
"Yeah sure Wally, I'll meet you at your car Dave. What is it Wally?". "It's a bit awkward mate, she had your phone number in her purse and I'm pretty sure it's your hand writing, she also had a diary on her, it detailed a relationship with you John and it goes into quite a lot of detail. John only I have seen this but you can imagine how this looks, I will destroy it if you wish". "Wally one drunken night I arranged to meet her and regretted it but I did take her out, we were heading to the Little Midget at Cramford Moor when DI Milton rang to tell me there had been a body found at Hangman's Gate which turned out to be Bethany Henshow so I

explained I had to take her back because that was work and I had to go back in, I took her back to the Spinning Jenny, I have not taken her out again and had no intentions either Wally". "You don't have to explain to me mate, we have been friends too long for me to doubt your word, I will destroy the piece of paper with your phone number and also the diary".

"Thanks Wally, I'd best get going". "Good luck John". "Come on John, what have you two been talking about? "Oh, something and nothing". They arrived at The Spinning Jenny, it was 11.30am and Wez was getting the bar ready for lunch time. "Flippin staff John, Laura didn't turn in last night and she is supposed to be doing a split shift today, I'm not happy

SMILE

mate, we gave her a job and a room because she said she didn't get on with her parents and this is how we are thanked". "Wez, can I stop you there, Laura has been found murdered near Shealdon" "Wez dropped the bottle of coke he was putting in the fridge, he went very pale. "Oh John, poor girl and there's me bad mouthing her, how bad am I?". "You were only blowing off steam mate, you didn't know".
"Carol Lestar is covering the bar for me John, I was just bottling up for her, I'd best go and tell Lindsay". "Wez ask Lindsay to get me Laura's parent's address, we'd best go and see them next". While he waiting he told Dave about Claire's theory. "John, I know she is an old friend but I find her ideas a bit off the wall" "Well you may well be right". Wez

came back with the address, he said
Lindsay was too upset. "No problem mate,
see you soon".
Laura Slooters address was Haddon
Manor in Youtgreave. "Sounds grand
John". They drove into Youtgreave and by
the old water tower in the village square
they stopped and asked lady directions. "I
know it well, I clean there, in fact I'm on
my way up there if you want to give me a
lift?" "Yes, jump in". They travelled about
half mile around the village then down a
long sweeping drive. "Do you walk here
every day?" "No, just Monday,
Wednesday, Friday and Sunday". "Blimey
that is some walk" the lady laughed at
Smarty's comments. The house looked
like an old Tudor mansion that had been

SMILE

added onto at various times, it was very impressive.

"Ok I'll tell Dorinda you have come to see her, who shall I say it is?" Detective Inspector Gammon and Detective Inspector Smarty". "Thought you would be Smarty" she said laughing as she left the car and headed into the house leaving them stood at the big oak door. "Wow this is some place" "It certainly is Dave". A lady came to the door. "Hi I'm Dorinda Slooter, how can I help you?". "May we come in please?" Gammon said, both showing their warrant cards. "Of course, come in". "Annie can you do us a pot of tea and some of those lemon crumbles chef makes please?".

Dorinda showed them into a magnificent drawing room with oil paintings everywhere. "Is your husband about Mrs Slooter?". "No I'm afraid he is in Dubai on a golfing holiday with some clients". "I'm afraid we have some bad news about your daughter Laura". "Yes, what about her? she has got some silly barmaid job at a pub, Mike isn't happy at all about that, what has she done now?" "I'm afraid she has been found murdered". Dorinda Slooter fell back onto the red leather Chesterfield settee sobbing uncontrollably, just then the lady called Annie came in with the tea. "Whatever is a matter Dorinda?" and she sat with her holding her trying to comfort her. "It's our Laura, she has been found dead".

"When is your husband expected back Mrs Slooter?" "Not for another week". "It's just, I am sorry to ask you this but the

SMILE

body will need formally identifying, we can arrange for an officer to pick you up tomorrow at 11.00 am". "No, I will bring Dorinda". "Thank you Annie". "Do you want me to arrange some counselling for you Mrs Slooter?". She said no in a very upset manner, "I live here Mr Gammon so I will take care of Mrs Slooter". "Ok, I am very sorry for your loss, here's my card, if you need anything just call me, day or night, anything at all, any friends that Laura had that you were uneasy with, anything at all Mrs Slooter". She nodded and carried on crying into her handkerchief.

"Worst part of the job John, it never gets any easier does it?" No it doesn't Dave, I wonder who Mr Slooter is?". "He's the owner of All Sports, they have shop's in every city". "Oh wow, he owns them does he? I can see where the money comes from then".

"Let's get back to the station". Gammon was met by a troubled looking Heather Burns. "Have you got a minute John?". "Sure, thanks Dave, see you in a bit". They climbed the stairs to DCI Burns office. "Shut the door John". "What is it Heather?" "I know you think I'm paranoid but I'm sure DS Cassells has been sent to spy on me". "Why are you thinking that?" Burns opened her draw and tossed a file on the table for John to read.

It was two pages of A4 paper. When he had finished reading it he agreed with Heather. "That's not good". "They are basically saying I am too soft with my staff, my ability to direct and get results

SMILE

are in question and so much more John".
"Look Heather, if it's any consolation, I
think you are a good copper, of course you
need time in the position and currently it's
a difficult time to be heading this up, DS
Cassells will only have tunnel vision, it
isn't personal, she expects results and they
expect that from her".
"We will get this lunatic, he will slip up"
"My only concern is we may have a
copycat because none of the others had
been sexually assaulted except Keri
Varney but she had just one scar from the
first attack and we have the man in
custody that sexually attacked her and
killed her".
"So, the pattern was no sexual contact,
now either the person is upping his game
or we have a copycat, either way he will

slip up and I will be waiting when he does".

"Don't let it get you down, the things the hierarchy have done to me over the years, it's a wonder I have a job or even want it, keep your chin up, a result is just around the corner". "Thank you" she said as John left her office. He stood with a coffee looking over beautiful Losehill knowing the writing was on the wall for Heather but how could he have told her that?

Why did the killer now sexually assault his victim? it didn't make sense unless he knew her or it was a copycat. John decided to call at the Spinning Jenny and have a chat with Lindsay, women notice things that men don't so it was better he spoke with Lindsay not Wez.

SMILE

John went onto the back-car park as it was 6.00pm and Lindsay would have been prepping in the kitchen. "Hi Lindsay, how are you?". "Oh, we have been so busy John, I did eighty-five meals at lunch and we have a party of twenty-six in tonight". "Could I ask you a few questions about Laura Slooter?". "Of course, how were her parents?" "Well her father was golfing in Dubai but we informed the mother". "I can't imagine how she must feel". "Did you know her parents were wealthy?" "I didn't at first but about a week ago I called at her room to see if she had any washing and she was crying on the bed". "Did she say why?" "Well she told me that her father was very rich and she was actually adopted, apparently he never had time for kids because he was always building the

sport shop business, it was her mother that
wanted children so she talked him into
adopting. She said when she was sixteen
she asked her mother, I think she said her
name was Dorinda?". "Yes it is Lindsay".
"Well she asked her if she minded trying
to find her biological mother, apparently
her father went ape, he said she was an
ungrateful cow, that they had taken her
from the gutter and given her a fantastic
life and now she wanted to go digging in
the gutter, that was when she had seen our
advert for live in staff and rang us.
She said her real mother had been a
junkie, she was told she lived in Bristol, I
felt so sorry for her, I said I would help
her find her natural mother, maybe I
shouldn't have done John but she seemed
so vulnerable, I couldn't just leave her like

SMILE

that. Wez doesn't know, not that I was
hiding it from him but we only started
looking a week ago". "Have you found
anything?" "No, not yet and now I
suppose there is no point anymore, that's
all I really know. Don't forget tomorrow
night bowling". "Lindsay I have so much
on at work I'm going to have to duck that
tomorrow". "Well don't forget Saturday
night we have Beavis the Joker disco".
"Isn't that the one Carol and Jimmy had at
their party?" "Yes, he was that good we
asked him to do a Saturday night here".
"Well I'll definitely come to that, please
explain to everyone about the bowling".
"Will do John". "Thanks, see you
Saturday".

John decided to go home and read the last bit of his book to get his head thinking clearly.

SMILE

Chapter 11

Nothing happened the following day at work, Heather was still all on edge and John decided to stay behind and get his paperwork bang up to date. He was glad he had ducked the bowling, for one he had played at a very good level and his competitiveness would have come out and it was just meant to be a bit of fun and two, he didn't fancy it if Saron was going to be there with Paddy.

He was back home at 8.30pm so just toasted some tea cakes made a strong coffee and went to bed with the final chapters of his book and of course DC. It was almost midnight when his mobile rang, it was Lindsay. "John, sorry to bother you so late but I remembered something, about four days ago we were having a coffee break and Laura asked me my opinion on a guy, she said he was older than her" Gammon had a shiver run down his back. "She said he was a bit creepy but was basically a nice guy". "Did she give you a name Lindsay?". "I did ask her and she said I would know him and she would point him out so I assumed he might be a local in the pub John". "I wonder, have you moved anything in Laura's room yet?". "No we haven't had time" "Ok well don't, I will pop over tomorrow and take a look, should be about 11.00 am" "That's fine John, I will be in the kitchen and I will give you a key". John hung up. One of his concerns was it appeared that she could have been talking about him. Did she consider him weird perhaps? Because of what Wally had

SMILE

found he needed to take a look at her room.

The following morning John got the key and started looking in her wardrobe and drawers, they were full of the usual young girl things then, in the bottom of the wardrobe was a box folder, John opened it and it was stuffed with letters, they were all saying the same thing, how much he loved Laura and how they should be together plus all sloppy stuff and they were all signed BJ.

It appeared Laura had kept them in date order but oddly, the oldest date on top, John counted thirty-three letters, it appeared she had received one every day. The last letter shocked him so he read it two or three times.

"My darling Laura,

You won't answer my dreams so I have to
make my dreams reality. Meet me in
Shealdon, just past the pub there is a field,
go through the stile and walk two fields up
and I will reveal who I am too you.
We will have such a fantastic time but you
have to see me to know this.
Look forward to seeing my beautiful
Laura
BJ xx"
John told Lindsay he would have to get
forensics up. "We won't disturb the pub
but we need to go through the room. I'm
taking these to work". "Yeah, whatever
John" poor Lindsay was so busy John
thought he could have said anything and
she would have said yes, she was
concentrating on cooking. John phoned
Wally and told him about the letters and

SMILE

asked if he could do a sweep of the room on Sunday. "Certainly can mate, in laws are over for lunch so great excuse, I owe you one". John could always rely on Wally no matter what.

Gammon went to the station much to the surprise of PC Magic, he grabbed a coffee and read every letter making notes as he went. This is the killer certainly of Laura and possibly the others. By the time it was 5.00pm he had a list as long as his arm of notes from this person to Laura, in them he mentioned a little something for you, John didn't know what that meant so was hoping Wally would turn up with something.

He called it a night, went home, showered and shaved then headed to the Spinning Jenny as promised. All the crew were in

and Bob was quite enjoying giving John
stick about his lack of bowling ability.
After ten minutes or so of this, Kev let it
slip about John playing at a very high level
as a kid which took the wind out of Bob's
sails.

The disco was in full swing as was the DJ
getting everybody dancing. John hadn't
spotted Saron which put a dampener on
his night then he realised she was with
Donna Fringe so he wandered over.

"Evening ladies, what's this, have you
shut for the night?" "No, we got staff in
this the first time, we have both had a
night out together, the first since we took
over the Tow'd Man". "Well it's good to
see you both, would you like a drink?"
"Can I have a large red wine please?"
"Donna what would you like?" "I'll have a

SMILE

double rum and coke please, thank you".
"Coming right up". It really was a
cracking night although didn't get much
chance to talk to Saron, he certainly
enjoyed himself. Donna said she would
drop him of on their way back to the
Tow'd Man, this suited John, he thought
he could walk back for his car Sunday and
see Wally at the same time.
The following day John set off, he
wondered about calling DS Cassells but he
really needed to crack this case for
Heather so she could take the credit then
hopefully there would be no more unrest
with another change of DCI at Bixton.
John arrived and asked Wally about the
letters saying they mentioned "there was
something for Laura" in some of them.

"Well we have found a box with four necklaces". "Wally, I have a hunch these are off the murdered girls, look at that one" John showed him a gold necklace with LT on it. "Ok John, take them but I'm not responsible for cross contamination" "Ok mate, you are a star". John headed straight to Rowksly and Lizzie Tuffs house at Stinton Terrace, he knocked loudly and Belmont answered. "Not you again, don't you ever give up?" "Craig, have you ever seen this necklace before?" "Yes, it's Lizzie's, she never took it off" "Great, thank you". "Hey, is that it?". "I hope so" Gammon said, getting in his car. Next, he went Churchtown Manor. Christina was at front of house, they were very busy with Sunday lunches. "Christina, I won't keep

SMILE

you long, there are four necklaces here, are any of the Bethany's?" "That looks like Beth's with the little padlock, she always said that's where she kept her heart. Where did you find it Mr Gammon?" "I will explain another time Christina but I have to get on". Gammon left hurriedly to go to Much's house but he wasn't keen on seeing Graham Much as he could still be the killer so he sat and waited, eventually Mrs Much came out to go to the shops and Gammon asked if any of the three necklaces could have been Chelsea's. "That one with Chelsea FC on it Mr Gammon, where did you find it?" "This is a bit unorthodox Mrs Much but I would appreciate you keeping our meeting a secret for now, I believe we are close to finding the killer". "Oh, ok Mr Gammon".

John was now convinced, with one to go, that whoever wrote the letter to Laura killed all these girls and Laura for whatever reason. John arrived at the Murrays and showed them the silver necklace with a large pearl as its centre piece, straight away Tamisha Murray said "That is Chloe's, her grandma sent it her. Where did you find it?" "Please just give me a few more days, we are close to catching the killer Mrs Murray". John left them and called Heather Burns, she was delighted, he said he had purposely kept DS Cassells in the dark and that Heather should take the glory because of the situation. He said he would see her tomorrow when hopefully Wally might have some DNA.

SMILE

John called at the Spinning Jenny and said what a good night he'd had. "I know the DJ can be a bit weird but he packs them in John". "Didn't watch him much to be honest". "I always think of Beavis and Butthead when I see him with him calling himself Beavis". "Yeah, I see what you mean mate".

The following day on the way to work Gammon called DS Bass and DI Milton. "Carl do you know here Beavis Joker lives?" "Yes, he has a remote farmhouse near Dumpling Dale". "Bring him in for questioning". "Ok John, on what?" "Anything, just think something up and I also want his house and out buildings, if he has any, getting a thorough search". Gammon went into the meeting. "Ok, this from yesterday's events, while you lot were sunning yourself over a pint no doubt, Wally what did you find?". "Sorry John, hardly anything other than an address with some DNA on it, we matched Laura Slooters DNA and we got a match again so it is somebody without a record I'm afraid". "Right, well I have Beavis Joker coming in, get yourselves over to his place at Dumpling Dale, anything you find phone me, I think he is our man".

Milton arrived with Beavis Joker, DS Bass did the tape. "Would you like a solicitor?" "No, I have done nothing wrong, what is this?". "Give me your full name please" "Beavis Joker" "So that is your real name?". "No, I was born Phillip Bould but changed it many years ago". "Did you know a Laura Slooter?" "She is that young barmaid at the Spinning Jenny, tidy little

SMILE

thing". "Write your initials on this piece of paper". He wrote BJ. Gammon looked at it then remembered on the front of his disco stand he had a big picture of Heath Ledger as the Joker and that is exactly how those poor girls looked.

The interview had been going almost an hour and Gammon knew this was the maniac. PC Magic knocked on the door, "Sir, I've got DI Smarty on the phone". "John, I have found a shed with a make - up bed and a chain on it, there is also a knife and pictures of all the victims from newspaper cuttings, he also had a table of events, next to each name is a picture of the Joker". "Bloody hell Dave, we have him, thanks mate, we are celebrating tonight".

Gammon went back in "I would suggest
Mr Joker that you have a solicitor present,
you can have one of your choosing or we
can supply a duty solicitor". "I haven't got
a clue what this is about".

"DS Bass, hold the tape there while I get
Mr Joker a solicitor".

Two hours passed and by now Wally was
back, he had the knife and it hadn't been
cleaned, it had traces of all the girls Joker
had murdered. "I think that's enough
Wally".

Gammon entered the room with duty
solicitor, Henry Gabbitt. "Ok Mr Joker,
we have reason to believe that you are the
person responsible for the murders of
Lizzie Tuffs, Bethany Henshow, Chelsea
Much and Chloe Murray, Laura Slooter
and the attempted murder of Keri Vaney.

SMILE

What do you have to say for yourself?"
"Its rubbish". Gammon showed him the
knife. "This knife has all of those girl's
blood on it, not only that, my officers
found a chart with these girl's names on it
next to a picture of the Joker and
newspaper cuttings about each case, I
suggest you start talking and quick Mr
Joker. Oh, before you do, we also found
the necklaces you kept from each victim
and sent with each letter, of which there
are thirty, to Laura Slooter".
At that Beavis Joker broke down, "It was
Laura's fault, I told her I would kill a girl
each time she turned me down". "So,
Laura Slooter knew you were killing girls
because of her?". "Yes" "And eventually
you killed her, why?" "Because I didn't
want to carry on killing anymore girls".

"Why did you cut their mouths?" "Well that way Laura knew the Joker had done it".

"Beavis Joker I am charging you with the attempted murder of Keri Vaney, the murders of Lizzie Tuffs, Bethany Henshow, Chelsea Much, Chloe Murray and Laura Slooter. You do not have to say anything but what you say maybe taken down in evidence and could be used in a court of law, do you have anything to say?". Beavis Joker stood up and started dancing and singing "Bye Bye Baby, Baby Goodbye" "Take him down to the holding cell". Gammon couldn't wait to tell Claire. "I think he is a fruitcake Claire and will probably be sectioned but at least he is off the streets hey?".

SMILE

"Well my work is done here John so I'm off back to London" "Are you not stopping for the celebrations in the Spinning Jenny?". "No, I will leave that to you and your confidante hey DCI Burns?" and she flicked her hair and left. "John, I don't know how to thank you". "All part of the service Heather" and he grinned. "You are a one-off John Gammon". "I have been called worse! The best bit of this job is the party tonight to celebrate". "Oh John I can't make it, I have to write this lot up and the sooner the powers that be get the good news the less stressed I will feel, trust me, but I will pay for this one, you paid for the last one, fairs fair". "Ok" "Are you going to ring Wez as well?" "Yes I'll do it now and I will tell Magic to inform the team". "Thanks

Heather". John retreated to his office feeling quite smug that it was a case closed.

The party at the Spinning Jenny was in full force when John arrived and to his surprise Saron was there. "Hey, where have you been?" "I've just finished work, surprised to see you here". "You have a lot of friends who care about you John Gammon and a little birdy rang me and said you were quite down". "Well you know how the job gets you sometimes, it was feeling like two steps forward three steps back, so who rang you?" "I'm not telling you yet but I'm here so let's enjoy ourselves". She looked stunning in an off the shoulder black mohair jumper with white tight trousers with black stiletto with the trade mark red sole meaning they were

SMILE

Christian Louboutin. John admired style, he had always liked fashion labels. Saron linked her arm in his and they walked over to DI Smarty and DI Milton who by now had quaffed three pints of Stella so were not slow with the comments. "Blimey John, how do you do it, the prettiest girl in Derbyshire and you just crack a massive case and this is all in one day". "You are blessed my son" and Smarty laughed. Milton smiled, John Gammon would always be his boss although their ranks were the same he was held in such high esteem at Bixton. "Put some music on Wez". "What do you want?"" Anything but I want a slow dance with my man at some point Wez" everybody cheered. John wasn't sure if he had heard Saron right, her man? This day can't get much better

can it he thought. She made him dance to
Abba which wasn't his favourite group
and he saw that Smarty and DI Lee, who
was also half cut by now, were dancing
behind them.

By nine, half of the police lads had gone,
Shelley and Jack came in with Tony and
Rita, they had been to see the latest film
about Churchill at Ackbourne cinema and
decided on a quick beer on the way home,
that wasn't going to happen now. Saron
was also getting a bit tipsy. She playful
chewed on John's ear "Are we staying at
yours tonight?" Blimey this was just too
good to be true he thought. "Yeah, yeah,
that would be great". She smiled like only
Saron could then tugged him onto the
dance floor to the Bryan Adams hit

SMILE

"Everything I do" John's heart was racing as she whispered the song into his ears. After the song it was almost 12.10am, Lindsay said she had done what Saron had said and booked a taxi and it was outside, she then passed John an overnight bag that Saron had bought. "Oh thanks Lindsay" and Saron and John headed for the taxi. When they got inside his kitchen he wanted to ravish her but DC came around. "Hello DC, have you been a good kitty for the big bad policeman? Just nipping to the bathroom John, give me a few minutes". I've got some red wine, shall I bring a bottle up and two glasses?" "Sounds great, put one in my room?" "Oh, are we not sleeping together?". "Not tonight lover boy".

John lay in bed totally confused, it was like Saron was playing a game with him, he decided over breakfast he would have it out with her.

The following morning he could smell bacon cooking, Saron was already up and dressed. "Morning John". "Morning, can we talk?" "Of course, what about?" "Last night". "Yes, I really enjoyed it John, you know how I love a dance". "No, I'm talking about when we got back here". "Ok, so what?" "Well, you slept in the spare room". "Is there a problem with that?" "It just confuses me, the big come on and then you sleep alone?"

"Sit down John, we need to talk. I went to the doctors yesterday". "Are you ok?" "Well, fifty- fifty to be honest, I'm

SMILE

pregnant". John spilt his coffee "You are? So why fifty fifty?" "Well I am over the moon, I am going to be a mum but", Saron stalled and cleared her throat, "I'm not sure if it's yours or Russell's".

"You have slept with Paddy?" "John, it was a drunken mistake, I knew you would be like this, I told Lindsay you would".

"What, you have told Lindsay about this?" "Yes, we have become good friends and she was the one that suggested to come last night"

"Oh great, who else knows? Have you told Paddy?" "No, I haven't" "Are you going too?" "John, I don't know, it can't be his I only slept with him once". "Bloody hell Saron, now we have a mess". "Don't you want to be a dad?" "Of course I do and if the situation was different I would be swinging from the chandeliers, I'll book a taxi, I need to get to work". "Already done, it should be here in five minutes". "John, you have always said you wanted stability with me so what's changed other than we will have a child together?". "Yes, but it's possibly not mine, that isn't what I want". Saron stood up as the taxi pulled up "I wish I hadn't told you, you are acting like a fool John Gammon".

Not a word was said as the taxi arrived at the car park, Saron got straight into her car and John did the same, she sped off.

John's drive to work it had him in a totally confused state, his emotions were in turmoil.

SMILE

What next Mr Gammon?

Printed in Great Britain
by Amazon